Country Love Story

Emily Worrell

Country Love Story

DEDICATION

I would like to say thank you to all my friends on so many platforms.

I have a lot of friends on social media, on twitch, and the at Starbucks. I would like to name some of my friends that are LBGTQ friendly. Without them friends being there for me I would have been in a really dark place or no longer here.

CONTENTS

	Acknowledgments	i
Chapter 1	Beautiful Brunette	1
Chapter 2	The Rodeo	7
Chapter 3	A Day at the Lake & The Oklahoma rodeo	12
Chapter 4	Valentine's Day	22
Chapter 5	Easter Sunday	30
Chapter 6	Childhood	43
Chapter 7	The Accident	48
Chapter 8	The Special Concert	56
Chapter 9	Summer Camp	62
Chapter 10	College Pride Event	72

Chapter 11   Engagement Party   84

Chapter 12   Wedding plans   94

Chapter 13   Veterans Day   103

Chapter 14   A hunting trip &   110

Thanksgiving

Chapter 15   The Wedding Day   123

Chapter 16   Christmas   133

Chapter 17   The Honeymoon   144

Chapter 18   Baby Fever   161

Chapter 19   Full of Surprises   169

Chapter 20   Birthday to Three   180

Chapter 21   The Ranch   188

ACKNOWLEDGMENTS

Very special thanks to my two counselors

Michael   Stephanie

Some special thanks to the people on social media

Kyle and Carol	Amanda	Marissa
Khloe	Carnie	Joann
Jacob	Christian	Eli

Want to thanks everyone on www.twitch.tv/

nanojade	KaysGameDays
Foxygen_Prime	maceplays
QuinnSolo	JudyDawn
Karlyy	Thegryphon
Cheezynerd	bristol242
tafgarcia	whitevelcro
whytlightnintv	ludacr0us
sammytraintv	keykaishouse
actiivevisiion	evaunalove
baronessvoncool7	grandpatitan

Chapter One

Beautiful Brunette

 Sweat dripped from their brows as Ryan and his best friend Luke practiced for the Houston Rodeo. It was getting near the end of August, and the rodeo was only weeks away. The temperature was one hundred four degrees outside. Ryan was sitting on Thunder, a champion bull, waiting for Luke to open the gate. With his rope wrapped tightly around his hand, Ryan braced himself. He knew he would need to stay on for at least six seconds to qualify. He gave a thumbs up with his free hand, signaling Luke to open the gate. Whoosh. The clock had started,

and Thunder was certainly not going to make staying on easy for Ryan. He kicked and bucked for all he was worth. Dust was flying up everywhere as Ryan struggled for balance. He noticed across the practice corral that he was being watched by a young brunette who looked absolutely stunning. At six and a half seconds, Ryan could hang on no more and found himself crashing to the ground. Seeing Thunder now charging after him, he got to his feet and made a run for the fence. Ryan quickly jumped over the fence. As he got to his feet, now safely away from the charging bull, he saw the young beautiful brunette wearing her white cowboy hat. Her long, wavy hair was gently blowing with the breeze. Ryan had never seen a woman so beautiful.

"You did great out there."

"That was my best run yet. Are you new around here, because I know I would have remembered a face as beautiful as yours?"

"I just moved here a few days ago. How often do you ride?"

"Luke and I practice twice a week. We switch off who rides

and who opens the gate. Today, it was my turn to ride, so next time it will be his. Well, I better go. I'm sure that Luke could use a hand getting Thunder back in his pen."

"Bye," called the brunette as she waved to him. As Ryan walked back over to where Luke was, he couldn't get this woman off of his mind. He told himself right then and there that if he ever saw this woman again that he would make it a point to try to get to know her. As he walked, his thoughts were suddenly interrupted as he heard his friend's voice.

"Dude, did you see that woman over there? She is smokin'. You've got to ask her out."

"I'll think about it," was all Ryan could say. He had been hurt in relationships before and was feeling hesitant about throwing himself fully at this woman. After his last breakup, Ryan had prayed,

"Lord, I can't do this anymore. Please, God, let the next woman I date be the right one."

With Thunder safely in his pen, Luke and Ryan headed for their trucks.

Luke asked, "Hey man, what do you say we go and grab a

beer? I don't know about you, but I sure feel like I could use one after being out in the heat all day."

"Sounds good to me! Meet you at the bar?"

And with that, they both got in their trucks. Ryan put on his seat belt and adjusted the radio. Ryan had decided that he would let Luke lead this time, as they peeled off splashing through some mud puddles left over from the water truck trying to keep the dust down. He was glad for a moment to just think to himself about everything going on in his life. Ryan had only moved to town about a year ago, after his last relationship had turned really sour. Divorce was never easy, but he did find some solace in the fact that he and his ex had never had any children together. His own parents had divorced when he was just a youngster, and he knew he would never want to see that happen to his own children. It had been a bitter divorce, and so he had moved here as a way of starting over. Ryan pulled into the parking lot. He was ready for that beer. Getting out of their trucks, Luke and Ryan headed inside the bar and waited in line to order their beers. A pre-season football game was playing on the TV, the Dallas Cowboys playing against the Denver Broncos. The

Cowboys were up ten to seven. The bar wasn't too crowded this time of day, and Luke noticed that one of the pool tables was open.

"Hey man, do you want to play?"

"Alright." As they made their way over to the pool table, Luke asked, "Do you want to rack 'em, or do you want me to?"

"I'll do it. You can break." Luke sat his beer down on the edge of the pool table and picked up the chalk. With his cue stick ready, he lined up his shot. Luke and Ryan both watched as the balls scattered, and, one at a time, one solid and two striped balls rolled into a pocket. "Great break!"

"Thanks, man! I call stripes. Say, if you ever see that woman again, even if you don't ask her out, do you think you could at least find the courage to get her name?"

Luke knew a little about Ryan's past and that it would take a little encouraging from a friend for him to work up the courage. He was well aware that Ryan was afraid of getting hurt again.

"Sure, I guess."

"Look, I know that you loved Stephanie and that the divorce was really hard on both of you, but don't let that stop you from trying to find love again. I think you should give this woman a shot. If you don't, then I will."

The two friends laughed, and then Ryan grew quiet and apparently was deeply in thought as he leaned over and took his shot. He watched as the cue ball rolled across the table and made direct contact with one of the solid balls; the ball landed in the corner pocket. Sensing that Luke would not let up about him getting back into the dating scene, Ryan finally consented to at least finding out her name if he ever came across her again. Taking a sip of his beer, Ryan relaxed as Luke's turn came again. Luke walked around the table, found the best angle, leaned over, and took his shot. As the game finished up, Luke and Ryan finished up their beers and left the bar.

Chapter Two

The Rodeo

The day of the rodeo had arrived. Ryan and Luke had been practicing for weeks on end for this day to come. As they are waiting for their turns to ride, Ryan couldn't help himself, but think back to that practice when he had seen that stunning brunette. As much as he had wanted to talk to her again and get to know her a little bit more, he had not seen her since that day. It was another hot day, and Ryan could feel the sweat trickling down his back as he waited for his name to be called. One of the rodeo's personnel signaled to him that he was now on deck.

As the dust stirred up under his boots, Ryan walked over to the bullpen and seated himself on the bull. He didn't know this bull, but all he knew was that he needed to get a good ride in and hang on as long as he could. Carefully, he wrapped the rope around his right hand and waited for his turn to begin momentarily. The bull snorted and pounded at the ground. As Ryan braced himself, he gave a thumbs up with his free hand. The gate swung open.

Whoosh.

The clock had started. The bull charged out, bucking and kicking, with Ryan trying desperately to hang on long enough to get a good time. About halfway through his ride, something caught his attention out of the corner of his eye. As the bull continued to buck, it was spinning Ryan in circles. He lost track of whatever had caught his attention, but then, he saw it again. This time, he was able to get a better look at it.

There was no doubt about it. The brunette he had met a couple of weeks ago while he was practicing was here watching him. Sensing that his distraction was having an effect on his balance, he redoubled his efforts to maintain his balance. The bull bucked and kicked, relentlessly trying to free itself from its unwanted rider. Finally, the bull achieved its goal, as Ryan felt the hard ground come crashing up underneath him, with dust flying everywhere. Getting to his feet, he knew when he got off the bull that he had no time to waste as the bull charged at him.

One wrong mistake and the bull could have put him in critical condition or even worse. Knowing that, Ryan ran to the fence. As he got to the fence, he slipped realizing that he made a mistake, but just in the nick of time, he got over safely. Just then, he felt someone bump into him. As he turned around, he saw her, every bit as gorgeous as he had remembered her from a couple of weeks ago. Ryan was determined not to let another opportunity pass him by.

Fumbling nervously for the right words to say, he simply said, "Hi, there."

He was all but drooling over this woman, and was it his imagination, or did this woman seem to drool over him as well?

"Hi there, handsome. You sure are looking good out there."

"Well, thank you, but pardon me, ma'am. I don't believe that I ever got your name."

"It's Emily,"

Ryan, feeling a bit stiff and sore after his ride, asked, "Would you want to walk around a bit?" Since this rodeo was part of the county fair, there was no shortage of things for them to see as the two of them walked and talked.

"I take it that you must be into rodeos?" he asked.

"Growing up, my dad owned a ranch in Austin. He used to take my brother and me to all the local rodeos. I think he was hoping that one of us would learn to love it the way that he did."

As they were passing by several food vendors, Ryan asked, "you thirsty? Can I buy you a drink?"

"Sure, I'll take a Bud Lite."

"So what brought you by the practice corral the other day?" Ryan asked as he handed her the drink.

"I live nearby. I had been out on a walk getting some fresh air when I heard you and your friend practicing."

The more Ryan and Emily talked; the more Ryan found himself wanting to know everything he could about this woman.

As they headed back to the rodeo stadium, he asked her for her number and said goodbye and headed off to find Luke. Even after saying goodbye, he could not stop thinking about her. Ryan caught up with Luke.6

"Hey, man. How'd you do?"

"The bull they gave me must've been the meanest one they had. I was barely able to hold on for five and a half seconds."

"Dude, that sucks! I made it to six seconds."

Chapter Three

A Day at the Lake

&

The Oklahoma Rodeo

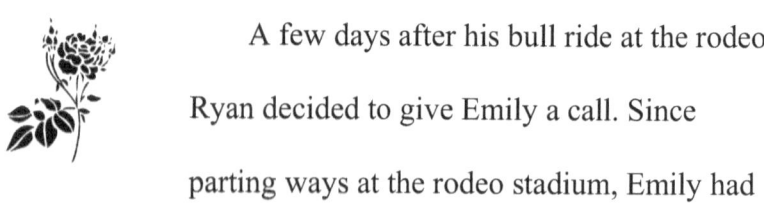

A few days after his bull ride at the rodeo, Ryan decided to give Emily a call. Since parting ways at the rodeo stadium, Emily had seemed to be all that Ryan could think about. He could feel that this was a totally different kind of love than what he had experienced with Stephanie. What he was feeling for Emily was more genuine. He picked up the phone and dialed her number. Then, he waited as he heard the answering machine.

"If you're calling about the horse, I sold it. If this is Thursday, I'm at the races. Wait for the tone. You know what to do."

As the answering machine beeped, he said, "Emily, this is Ryan. We met at the rodeo a couple of days ago. I wanted to know if you had any plans for Saturday."

Emily was at home unpacking some boxes for her parents, when she heard the phone ring. She looked at the caller ID but didn't recognize the number so she had let the answer machine pick up. When she heard Ryan's voice come on, her heart leapt. Ever since that day at the Rodeo, she had been hoping that he would give her a call and ask her out. She immediately ran to the phone and dialed his number.

"Hello."

"Ryan? This is Emily."

"Hey, Emily. I just tried to call you."

"Sorry about that! I've been busy, still trying to get all settled in, and I couldn't find where I had left the phone."

"No worries. You found it now. I actually was calling to see if you had any plans for Saturday."

"I'm completely free."

"Great! I'll pick you up about eleven. Wear something comfortable. You may want to bring a swim suit."

"I can't wait. See you in the morning."

Ryan had visited Lake Houston many times as a kid and wanted to take Emily there. The lake was a beautifully wooded area, surrounded by tall pine. To spot wildlife wasn't uncommon there, either. He was planning to surprise Emily with a picnic lunch by the water. Feeling like a kid on Christmas Eve, Ryan could barely sleep that night. He was so ready to see Emily again. Rising early, Ryan got out of bed and stumbled into the bathroom to take a shower. Still not quite awake, he undressed and turned the water on in the shower. He gave it a minute for the water to get warm and then stepped in the shower.

Water rained over his body as he shampooed his hair. This was just what he needed to wake up in the morning. All washed up, Ryan stepped out of the shower and grabbed his towel and dried off. As he threw on his well-worn jean shorts and his favorite t-shirt, he thought about what he would pack for lunch. He headed into the kitchen and made chicken salad sandwiches and wrapped them up. He packed them in a picnic basket with the plates, glasses, and silverware. Since he didn't have anything to go with the sandwiches, he loaded the picnic basket into his truck and got in. The dust stirred under the tires as he drove off to the store. Once there, he picked up some fresh fruit salad, chips, and a six-pack of beer.

He now had everything he needed for a picnic at the lake. He took his items to the cash register and paid for them. Walking out to his truck, Ryan put the food in his picnic basket. He could hardly wait to get to Emily's house. Ryan was so excited that it seemed like getting to her house took forever. In reality, it probably only took about five minutes or so. He pulled into her driveway, undid his seat belt, and got out of the truck.

Feeling excited and full of confidence, Ryan knocked on her door. Emily opened the door, and Ryan couldn't help himself. He whistled under his breath. She seemed to look fabulous in anything. Since he had told her to wear something comfortable, she had chosen a pair of her old, cutoff jean shorts, and a navy-blue tank top. Her hair was pulled back into a simple ponytail, and she wore flip flops. Emily greeted him with a hug, and Ryan knew that this would be a great day.

"Howdy! Are you ready to go?"

"I sure am. So where are we going?"

"I'm not telling. It's a surprise"

"Oh really, well then, let's get on with it. I want to find out where we are going."

Ryan walked Emily to his truck and opened her door for her. As he helped her climb inside, he couldn't help but notice her butt, barely covered by her shorts, a sight any man would love to behold, and for now, it was all his. With Emily safely seated in his truck, Ryan closed the door and walked around to his side of the truck. Opening his door, he hopped up in his seat and buckled up. He still felt giddy inside as he thought about the great day they would have. Putting the key in the ignition, he started the truck and put in a CD, Brad Paisley's "*Mud on the Tires*" started playing. With that, Ryan backed his truck out of Emily's driveway and began making his way to Lake Houston. Knowing it would be a bit of a drive until they reached their destination,

Ryan told Emily to settle in and enjoy the ride. He couldn't

believe his ears when Emily started singing along to the CD. She

had the voice of an angel. She sang right along with the whole

song and didn't miss a single word. Trees gradually replaced

buildings as they grew nearer to their destination. The whole

time, Emily hardly said a word, seeming to prefer to watch out

the window to figure out where he was taking her. In what had

seemed like no time at all to Ryan, they arrived at the lake.

Pulling into the parking lot, he couldn't help but notice that there

were very few other cars in the parking lot. This would only

make it easier for them to find a perfect picnic spot where they

could still feel kind of alone.

Well, this is it. We're here." Ryan said as he put his truck in

park and turned off the engine.

Sucking in a huge breath of the pines that filled the air,

Emily looked around. She couldn't believe how gorgeous this

place was. With the exception of a lone fishing boat a ways off

from the shore, the water was perfectly still. A little ways down

the shore from where they stood, a couple of kids could be heard

playing and splashing in the water. Looking down the shore in the other direction, an older looking man appeared to be looking relaxed as he waited for a fish to bite. Other than that, the lake was theirs for today.

"How about that spot right over there, by the dock? That seems like a great place to enjoy a picnic."

"Looks great to me," Ryan said as he carried the picnic basket over to the chosen spot. Emily had carried the blanket for him, and as she got to the spot, she stopped and spread the blanket out, so that Ryan could set the picnic basket down.

Ryan asked, "Would you likes to go to the Chesapeake Energy Arena Rodeo in Oklahoma City, Oklahoma?"

Emily replied, "I would love to. When is the rodeo?"

Ryan replied, "It's in January on a weekend." With that, they spent the night together, sitting under the clear night sky enjoying the view of the stars until the early morning, where they finally went home.

Time came, for the rodeo in Oklahoma and Ryan went by Emily's house to pick her up. When Ryan pull up to Emily's house, he got out and walked to the door and knocked on it. Emily's step father Mr. Luce, opened the door and said "Hi

Ryan. Why don't you come in? Emily is almost ready." Mr. Luce

and Ryan talked while Ryan waited for Emily get ready. After

about ten minutes passed, then Emily came down, and she

looked so beautiful in her country clothes. They both walked to

the car, and Mr. Luce told them to have fun but not to much.

When they got to the car, Ryan opened the truck door for Emily.

She got in and Ryan got in after her, and they both were off to

Oklahoma for the rodeo.

They played country music and talked the whole time going

to Oklahoma City, and they saw some cool things on the road

while they were on the road. After about three and a half hours,

and they both realized they hadn't eaten anything, so they drove

into a fast food place to pick up something to eat and get back on

the road. After another three hours, they made it to Oklahoma

City. They stopped at the hotel and got two rooms for Thursday

through Sunday. Then, they unpacked their stuff and went out for

the evening. Later, they came back and went to sleep, because

Ryan had the rodeo for the next three days.

The next morning, they got ready and went to the arena

where the rodeo was and signed up before it started. They had about six hours before the rodeo started, so they went to The National Cowboy & Western Heritage Museum for some western history, art, and culture, and they did lunch afterward. Then they went to the arena to do the rodeo. Ryan and Emily was talking and cheering on the other people until it was Ryan's turn to ride. Ryan was up now, and he was going to ride Call of the Wild, and Ryan let them know he was ready. They opened the gate, and they were off. Ryan got a time of seven point two.

Then Ryan jumped off the bull and ran, and hopping over the gate.

Emily came over to kiss Ryan and said, "You were great out there!"

After the show was over, Ryan and Emily went back to the hotel and got some sleep. On day two, and they both woke up, got an early dinner and went to the arena. Ryan was getting ready for his turn to ride. It had been over an hour, and it was Ryan's turn to ride again. He was on the bull called Time-breaker, and he got a time of six point seven. That put him for the last day ride, so they both went and got some sleep.

The two woke up early on the last day and went to the

museum of The Museum of Osteology, which displayed

hundreds of skulls and skeletons from all over the world. After

that, took over six hours to look at everything in the museum.

Then they got a bite to eat and went to the last day of the rodeo.

This time, Ryan got to ride Voodoo Child and got seven seconds.

He got off and ran to the gate and got over before the bull hit the

gate. After it was all over, they went and got sleep for the drive

home in the morning.

Chapter Four

Valentine's Day

 Luke and Ryan had been at the practice corral all morning, getting ready for when bull riding season came up.

Luke looked at Ryan and asked, "So, you have any plans with Emily on Valentine's Day?"

Ryan said, "Yea, bud, we got the whole day and night planned out".

"Luke, what are your plans for Valentine's Day?" Ryan

asked.

"Well, Ryan," Luke said, "I think I will just go and practice some more, then go to the bar and hang out." After that, they were done for the day and they went to put the equipment and the bulls up.

Luke said, "Good luck to Emily and you on your date."

" Thanks, Luke, and I hope you find a girl for you," Ryan said.

With that, both Luke and Ryan left to get some sleep for Valentine's Day tomorrow. Valentine's Day came, and Ryan got up around 10:00 A.M. and started getting ready for the date at noon. Ryan kept thinking to himself, *What can I get her today for Valentine's Day?* At 10:30 A.M., he went to Wal-Mart to see what they had for Valentine's Day gifts. He saw this cute bear with a heart shaped pillow on it, which had a cute poem on it that said, "Between sunset and sunrise, a musical force tells me. You are thinking about me as I'm thinking about you. With that, I look into the clear skies, where I can see the beautiful stars, and I found you coming from the heavenly skies, looking like an angel being with your love. Then, you give me a hug, and through that hug, I can feel your love and compassion."

So Ryan got the bear and shopped some more. Ryan came across some candy, the candy was a milk chocolate and white chocolate mix. Then, he saw the display of flowers at and he found the red roses with a pink top. He got a dozen of them. He made his way to the cashier to pay. At 11:20 in the morning, time had come to go pick up Emily. He drove to Emily's house and when he got there, he got out of the car with the flowers, candy, and the bear, and walked to the door. He knocked on the door, and she opened the door.

Emily said, "Hi, Ryan! Are those for me?"

Ryan was speechless, because of the way she looked. Emily had on this beautiful red dress with high heels on her feet, and her hair was all done up.

Ryan answered her, "Yes, these are for you, and you look like an angel."

"Why, thank you, Ryan. You look handsome yourself." Emily said, and Ryan started to blush. Emily giggled a little and said, "What do you have planned, my love?"

Ryan said, "First, I thought we would go see a movie, then

go get some dinner. After that, we can go do what you like to do." Emily and Ryan got in the truck and headed to the movie theater. When they got to the movie theater, Ryan asked Emily "What movie would you like to see?"

Emily said "How about the movie called *Endless Love*"

Ryan replied "OK, my love." Ryan asked the ticket guy, "Two tickets for *Endless Love*, please,"

"Ten dollars, please." Ryan paid for the tickets, and both Emily and Ryan went into the theater. Ryan asked Emily, "Would you like some popcorn and something to drink?"

Emily said, "No popcorn. Just a Dr Pepper, if they have it"

Ryan said, "OK, beautiful!" Ryan turned to the lady at the counter and said, "Two Dr Pepper's, please."

The lady at the counter said, "That will be nine dollars, Sir." Ryan handed the lady the nine dollars and took the drinks. Emily and Ryan went to the theater room where the movie was playing to find seats. About half way through the movie Emily grabbed Ryan's hand and held it for the rest of the movie. When the movie was over at 3:30 P.M., Emily and Ryan left the theater and went to Ryan's truck. As Ryan was pulling out of the parking lot, Emily asked Ryan,"Where are we going to go have dinner?"

Ryan said "It's a surprise, my love." With that, Ryan drove to a restaurant called *Barn Door.*

When they got to *Barn Door*, Emily said, "Oh Ryan, I love this steakhouse." Ryan parked, and Emily and Ryan went into the restaurant.

When they got inside, the host said, "I will be right with you."

Ryan said "OK."

About ten minutes later, host came by and asked them, "Is it just the two of you?"

Ryan told the host, "Yes, the two of us"

Then the host said, "Right this way." Ryan and Emily followed the host to their table and sat down, and the host asked, "May I get you something to drink?"

Emily answered "Dr Pepper for me."

"And for you, sir?" the host asked,

Ryan said, "I will have the same."

Then Emily and Ryan looked at the menu, and the waitress

came by and said, "I am going to be your waitress today, and my name is Sarah. Are you guys ready to order?"

They said, "Yes, we are."

Emily said, "I will have the fillet mignon, well done, and a baked potato, with chives, sour cream, and butter."

Then the waitress said, "And for you, sir."

Ryan told the waitress "I will have the porterhouse, medium well, and a baked potato, with chives, sour cream, and butter." The waitress walked off. Ryan and Emily talked about the movie that they just seen and about their families. About fifteen minutes later, Sarah came back with the food and refilled their drinks. While Emily and Ryan ate, they talked some more. About an hour later, they got done eating, paid the bill, and left a good tip.

Ryan asked Emily, "What would you like to do?"

Emily said, "Well, how about going to the lake and watching the stars together?"

Ryan said, "That would fun." So they hopped in the truck to go to the lake. When they got to the lake, it was just about night time. They both got out of the truck and put a blanket down, and they both lay there, holding each other. It now night time, a clear dark night, and you can see the stars. The two lay there, looking at the stars, and then they both said at the same time, "Did you just see those shooting stars?" Then they both giggled.

Then Emily said to Ryan, "Ryan, I love you, and I love this day, and the gifts, flowers, and the candy you got me."

Ryan said to Emily, "I love you too, and you're welcome, my dear." They started kissing. Ryan asked Emily, "Would you like to go to the bar and get some drinks?"

"Sure" said Emily. They got up and put away the blanket and got into the truck. When they got to the bar, they saw Luke outside, and Ryan dropped Emily off at the door and parked the truck. Ryan got out and went up to Luke.

"How's it going bud?"

Luke said, "Going good dude! How are Emily and you do on your date?"

Ryan said, "It was good. We went to the movies, then to dinner, then went to the lake and watched the stars. How was your day, Luke?"

Luke said, "It was good, just went and practiced and came to the bar." So Emily, Luke, and Ryan were at the bar, having some Bud Lights.

Luke asked Ryan and Emily, "Would you guys like to have a shot with me?"

Ryan and Emily said, "OK."

Luke called the bartender named Cindy over and told her, "May I get three shots, please?"

Cindy asked, "What would you like?"

Luke said, "Two whiskeys and apple cobbler."

Cindy said, "OK, and that would be eighty-two dollars and fifty cents. No fifty dollars."

Emily, Ryan, and Luke took the shots and called Cindy back and asked her, "May we please get three Bud Light's."

Cindy said "That would be nine dollars." They drank their beers, and they left a twenty-dollar tip. They all hugged goodbye.

"Bye Cindy!"

Cindy said "Bye." Then Ryan took Emily home.

Chapter Five

Easter Sunday

 Emily called Ryan at seven o'clock in the morning and asked, "Good morning, Ryan. What are you doing this morning?"

Ryan said, "Morning, Emily! Nothing too much."

Emily asked, "Would you like to come to church with me and my family?"

Ryan said, "Sure, I would like that! What time does it

start?"

,Emily said, "Bible class starts at 9:00 A.M., and worship starts at 11:00."

Ryan said, "I will meet you guys there."

Emily said, "OK." After telling Ryan where the church was, they both hung up the phone. Ryan went and got ready for Emily's church. He put on his nice dress clothes and his nice dress boots and headed to the church. When Ryan was heading to the church, he saw a lady on the side of the road, broken down. It was about one hundred five degrees outside. Ryan pulled over to see what was wrong with the car. He saw three kids in the back: a ten-year-old girl, a four-year-old girl, and a one-year old boy. The lady talked to Ryan while Ryan looked at the car.

The lady said, "I am from out of town and coming to see my family at River View Assembly of God."

Ryan said, "Sure funny, because that is exactly where I am going to right now." The lady asked about the car, and Ryan said, "Your fan belt is broken, and if you like, I can give you and your kids a lift to the church."

The lady said, "God bless you, Ryan!"

The lady and her kids got into Ryan's truck and went to the church. When they got to the church, Ryan dropped them off at the front of the church and parked his truck. Ryan got out and it was 9:25 A.M. He started to the class, and when he got there, he was five minutes late. He went to sit by Emily. After class was over, Emily asked Ryan, "Why were you late?"

Ryan said, "When I was on my way here, I saw a lady with three kids broke down, and I pulled over to see what was wrong. The lady said that she was out of town and was going to River View Assembly of God to meet up with family, so I brought then to the church."

Emily said, "That's why I love you Ryan!" So Ryan and Emily went to worship and found Emily's parents. The time was a little early for worship to start and Emily saw her cousin Ann.

She told Ryan, "This is my cousin, Ann." Ryan and Ann looked at each other, then smiled, and Emily look confused.

Emily asked Ryan and Ann, "Do you guys know each other?"

Ryan turned to Emily and said, "That is the lady I told you I helped out, not knowing it was your cousin!"

Then Ann said to Emily, "This is the Ryan you were telling me about!"

Emily said, "Yes, Ann! That is my baby that I'm going to marry!"

Ann said to Emily, "I can see why! He is a very good man, and God bless him!" Now it was time for worship service, and they were singing. One of the songs called, *"I Will Rise,"* started to make Ryan tear up and Emily saw him and gave him a tissue. Now, the entire music stopped and the preacher was talking about the Lord and how Easter was the time of the resurrection of the Lord. After the preacher finished talking, he asked if anyone wanted to come up and be saved by the Lord, and everyone started singing.

Ryan walked up and told the preacher, "I would like to be saved by the Lord." The preacher said a prayer for Ryan and then sent him to the back to set up to be baptized. Emily already knew where Ryan was, and she waited for him in the lobby.

When Ryan came out, Emily gave him a kiss and said, "I'm proud of you, Ryan for wanting to be saved."

So Ryan and Emily went to meet up with her parents at the

house. Emily's parents and Ann was waiting for them to start the Easter egg hunt for Ann's kids. When Ann and Emily's mother were making Easter dinner, Emily and Ryan went to hide the eggs while Mr. Luce was watching the kids. When Emily and Ryan were done hiding the eggs. They went inside the house and told the kids that they could go find the eggs. Emily took the kids out to find the eggs while Mr. Luce and Ryan talked. After about an hour, the kids and Emily came back inside, put a movie on for the kids, and then went to help out Ann and her mother with dinner. After thirty minutes passed, Ryan went into the kitchen to help set the table. After the table was set, Mrs. Luce called everyone to the table, and when everyone was there, Mr. Luce said a prayer before they started eating.

Mr. Luce said, "Dear Lord, bless our food on this special day. Let it bring nourishment to our bodies as you nourished our spirits. Today, Heavenly Father, as we enjoy our meal, we first take the time to forgive all those who may have hurt us or sinned against us. Just as you showed grace and mercy to the world, we also show grow and mercy to everyone in our lives. Thank you, Father, for this time together. Amen."

After Mr. Luce finished saying the prayer, everyone said, "Amen," and they all started eating. When everyone was done eating, Ann went and put a movie on for the kids and went back into the kitchen to help put away the food. Mr. Luce and Ryan got to where the car was and changed the belt. Ryan got in the car and brought it back to the house. The two men went in the house and sat down.

Emily said to the men, "Dad and baby, would you like some pie?"

They both said, "Sure," So Emily brought them both some pie, and everyone was in the living room.

They were all talking for hours and Ryan said, "Thanks for everything, Mr. and Mrs. Luce, Emily, and Ann. I got to be heading home myself."

Everyone said, "Your welcome."

Ann said to Ryan, "Thanks for everything you did for me today."

"You're welcome, Ann," said Ryan, and with that, Emily walked Ryan to his truck. Ryan gave Emily, a big kiss and said, "I had a very nice time, and I love you very much, my dear."

Emily said, "I love you too Ryan." As she turned and went back to the house, Ryan left for home. As Ryan was on his way home. The night was dark and the road was really foggy. He turned on the radio station called *K–LOVE* to help him stay calm through the thick fog. He went back to driving, and while he was driving, the front tire on his truck blew out half way home. When the tire blow out, the truck started to get out of control.

Ryan started praying to the Lord saying, "Dear Lord, help me to safely and in one piece!" All of a sudden, the truck started to slow down and now was on the side of the road. Ryan thanked the Lord and got out of the truck and started looking around. He looked at the tire and said, "Oh man! Where am I?" Ryan heard some howling of coyotes off in the distance. Ryan was thinking to himself, *"I'm going to get my tire changed and get out of this area."* About five minutes later, he started to get the stuff out to change his tire. Then, Ryan heard a different howling close by. Ryan got a little scared but went back to getting the stuff out. After about three minutes, the howling was getting really close, and Ryan dropped what he was doing and got into the truck.

He tried calling his friend Luke, but there was no cell

service where he was. Ryan heard a noise outside of the truck, and he looked up to find a pack of wolves about ten of them, circling the truck, trying to get in to the truck. The only thing Ryan could do was to pray to the Lord for help. About fifteen minutes later, Ryan saw some headlights coming up to him. When the white four by four F–350 stopped, Ryan could hear gunshots go off from the white truck, and all the wolves ran away.

The older man got out of the truck and walked up to Ryan and asked, "Are you OK."

"Yes, and thank you, sir, for scaring off the wolves," said Ryan.

The old man asked Ryan, "What are you doing out here?"

Ryan told him, "I was on my way home, and my tire blew out."

The old man helped Ryan change out his tire, and the old man told Ryan, "It's not safe driving this road on a foggy night. You can stay at my house until the fog lets up, and by the way, my name is Bob Cola"

Ryan said, "Thank you very much. My name is Ryan."

After the tire was fixed, Bob had Ryan follow him home, and when Ryan was following Bob, Ryan was thinking, *Where have I heard that man's name before?* About twelve minutes later, they both made it to Bob's house and parked their trucks and went into the house. Then Bob got some things for Ryan to sleep in, and Bob went to bed. Ryan was looking at Bob's things on the wall and thought, *Could it be! Could Bob be Eaglewolf, the professional bull rider. The best of all time.*

Ryan was tired and thought his mind was playing tricks on him, so Ryan lay down and went to sleep. In the morning, he smelled something really good, so Ryan got out of the bed, put his boots on and went to the kitchen. He found Bob making breakfast. There were pancakes, hash browns, sausage, bacon, eggs, and toast. Bob saw Ryan and said, "Pull up a chair, and have breakfast with me."

Ryan said, "OK, and thank you, Bob." While they were eating, Ryan asked, "Bob, can I ask you a question?"

Bob said, "Sure."

"Were you a bull rider before?" Ryan asked.

Bob said, "I was at one time, and I am retired now. Why

do you ask."

Ryan said, "Because you look like the man that people called Eaglewolf. The whole town where I live tells stories of Eaglewolf and how he was a legend in the whole bull riding sport."

"Well, Ryan, I was a legend, and yes, Eaglewolf was my nickname." The look on Ryan's face was priceless.

Ryan told Bob, "Bob, I too am a bull rider, and I got into bull riding because of the stories of you. You're my hero."

Bob said, "Thank you! Do you want to show me what you know? Then, I could teach you what I know."

Ryan said, "Sure! This will be fun! I enjoy learning new things." So, with that, Ryan and Bob went out to a practice corral. Bob went to go get some bulls, and Ryan felt like a little kid again.

When Bob got back with the bulls, Bob said, "I got four bulls you can ride. The first one's name is Raging Volcano. Second one's name is Thunderbolt. The third one's name is Quick Lightning, and the last one's name is Tornado."

"Cool," Said Ryan.

"So the first one you'll ride will be Tornado" said Bob. With that Ryan got Tornado rigged up and Bob was waiting for the sign from Ryan. About three minutes later, Ryan gave Bob the sign, and Ryan was out of the corral on Tornado, turning one way real fast, Then the other way, and then Ryan fell down after four seconds.

Bob said, "That looked good, but I saw some things wrong when you were out there."

"What was I doing wrong out there, Bob?" Ryan asked.

Bob told him, "You see, when you went out, you were okay, but when the bull started to jump, you loosened your legs, and your hand went down. The tighter your legs are against the bull, with your hand up for balance. Here, let me show you on Quick Lighting, Ryan."

"OK," said Ryan, and with that Bob got up on Quick Lightning and gave Ryan the sign. Quick Lightning jumped out in the corral and leapt three feet off the ground then turned and bucked and when Ryan waved his hands, Bob let go of the harness and fell off the bull. When Bob got back to Ryan, Ryan said, "Bob, you were really great out there, and I see what you mean about the legs and my hand."

Bob asked Ryan, "Would you like something to drink?"

"Sure, Bob" said Ryan So Bob and Ryan went to the house and got some sweet tea. After they got done, Ryan and Bob went back out to the corral, and Ryan rode the other two bulls that were left.

"Hey Bob, I had fun spending time with you! Thanks again for the pointers and scaring off the wolves," said Ryan

"No problem, Ryan. Here is my number, Ryan, and let me know the next time you compete," Bob said.

"OK," said Ryan and with that, Ryan said bye to Bob and drove home. When he got home, he got out of the clothes he was wearing and got cleaned up, put on some comfortable clothes and called Emily.

Emily picked up the phone and said, "Hello."

"Hello dear. I'm home now," said Ryan.

Emily said "Oh thank God! I was worried something might have happened to you." Ryan told Emily everything that happened from his tire blow-out to meeting the man with the nickname of Eaglewolf.

Emily said, "Thank God for that man coming out when he did, and by the way, what was the man's name?"

Ryan told her, "His name is Bob Cola."

"You mean the legendary Bob Cola, the professional bull rider of all times? That Bob Cola?" said Emily.

"Yes, dear, that Bob Cola!" said Ryan.

"Cool!" Said Emily

"Well, dear, I'm going to get off this phone and get some sleep," said Ryan.

"OK, and I love you, baby," said Emily

"I love you too, beautiful." said Ryan, and with that, they both got off the phone, and Ryan fell asleep.

Chapter Six

Childhood

Later that day Emily got a phone call from a number she didn't know, so she picked up and said, "Hello?"

"Hey, Emily!"

"Who is this?"

"This is your father, Tim." The look on Emily's face was like she was going to cry.

Emily said, "Hi," with the sound of wanting to cry.

Tim said, "Why do you sound like your going to cry? I

didn't raise no cry baby. I called you, because I have stage four cancer and don't think you're going to get anything from me." He said some other stuff too, but Emily cut him off by hanging up the phone. She started crying, and the phone began ringing again. Emily didn't pick up but sent it to voice-mail and continued to cry a lot more. Then, Emily's mom walked by her room and heard Emily crying. She walked into the room. Emily's mom asked, "What wrong, Sweetie?"

"It was Tim."

"Oh, sorry, Sweetie! Come give Momma a hug!" Emily slid to her mom and gave her a hug. After a ten-minute hug, Emily's mom had to go to work, and Emily went back to crying. Emily cried for three hours straight and then called Ryan, still crying.

Ryan pick up the phone and said, "Hello, sweetie."

"Hey, dear," she answered in a sad tone

"What wrong?"

"It's my dad, he's being a jerk, right now."

"Mr. Luce is?"

"No, Mr. Luce is my step father. I'm talking about my

biological father Tim. Can you come over"

"Give me twenty minutes, and I will be there."

"OK," They hung up their phones. Emily heard the doorbell and let Ryan in. Before Ryan could make it through the door, Emily just hugged him and didn't want to let go. After ten minutes, Emily let go, and they went up to her room to chat.

Once in her room, Ryan asked, "So why is he being that way?"

"Well, let me tell you how I grew up. The whole time, I was growing up my dad was always verbally abusive to me. He would always say, I am nothing and mean stuff. If I helped out around the house, I always got yelled at, and if I didn't do anything, I got yelled at, and if I got good or bad grades in school, I got yelled at. My sister disowned the whole family after she got married, just to get away from our dad, and I was only sixteen at the time. If I did anything good, my dad turned it into something negative and made me feel like crap. When I came out as a trans-gender female at the age of twenty-six, my dad got really verbally abusive at me and said, that no guys like a fat chick, and I was average size back then. I didn't start working out until my mom left Tim. Today, Tim my biologically dad called me up and said, that he has stage four cancer. Then he told me that I wasn't going to get anything from him when he passed away and told me why should I line your pockets with anything, since you didn't line my pockets. I couldn't take it anymore and hung up with him."

Ryan looked at Emily and asked,"So, what age did you know that you were different."

"I was ten years old when I knew that I was different. At the age of thirteen, I snuck into my sister room and tried on her clothing. I felt more myself with my sister's clothing on. In school, I didn't have any friends, because I was bullied growing up. It got worse in high school, because I didn't know how to fit in. I didn't fit in with the guys, because I didn't know guy talk, and I couldn't tell some of the guys that I liked them. I didn't fit in with girls, because the girls saw me as a guy and didn't want to hangout. I got bullied by the high school staff and peers. I was depressed for sixteen years before I came out, and I was happy I did. At the age of twenty-seven, I started Hormone Replacement Therapy, and at the age of twenty-eight, I had my Gender

Reassignment Surgery, and I was really happy, because I was more myself."

Then Ryan asked, if Emily could have kids, and she told him that she had put a uterus in, when she had her surgery done. Emily added, "If you are not OK with my past, I would understand."

"The past is the past, and I didn't fall in love with the past you, I fell in love with the now you and who you are now." Emily put a movie in the DVD player and lay down on the bed. she looked at Ryan and just snuggled up against him, while he put his arms around her and held her tight. They watched the movie. Emily fell asleep in Ryan's arms and he stayed with her until she was okay. Every time Ryan tried to get up, Emily started to wake up, so Ryan stayed in her bed, holding her until the morning.

When Emily's mom got home, she checked up on Emily and saw Ryan and her asleep and said to herself, "I hope Ryan is the one, because my little girl has been through a lot in life," and she turned and went to her room and fell asleep.

Chapter Seven

The Accident

 Ryan didn't think anything of the missed phone call at the time and just assumed that Emily just wasn't home or something. Ryan would find out all too soon just why she didn't answer his call. Later that evening, Ryan, sitting at home completely comfortable in his pajama bottoms and t-shirt, was watching the news. As he watched, he felt his heart nearly fall to the floor. As far as he was concerned, it was as though the world had simply stopped moving in that moment. The news had just aired a story about a head on collision that had happened that afternoon.

In a desperate attempt to identify one of the victims, Houston Police Department had decided to air her picture in hopes that somewhere, someone would recognize this woman. There was a number to call scrolling across the screen for anyone who had any idea about this woman's identity. Ryan picked up the phone and dialed the number that scrolled across the screen. An officer answered the phone.

"Houston Police Department, Officer J. Smith. How can we help you?"

"Yes, my name Ryan, and that's my girlfriend Emily on the TV screen."

The officer said, "Your girlfriend is in the hospital. A drunk driver hit her head on, and she is in critical condition and in a coma."

Ryan said, "OK, thank you, Officer Smith." The next day, around 9:00 A.M. Ryan went to the hospital.

The front secretary asked, "May I help you, Sir?"

Ryan said, "Yes ma'am, I am looking for Emily Luce."

Then the secretary asked, "Are you a family member?"

Ryan said, "No, I'm Emily's boyfriend, and her parents are

out of the country."

The secretary said, "OK, she in the ICU."

Ryan said, "OK, thank you, ma'am."

When Ryan got to the ICU, the nurse asked Ryan, "Hi, may I help you?"

Ryan, in a sad and nervous voice, said, "Yes, I'm looking for my girlfriend Emily Luce."

The nurse said, "Emily's right over here, and my name is Norma. If you need anything, come get me."

Ryan said, "OK."

Then Ryan walked up and just started crying right there and said, "Emily, I am here, my love." Ryan went outside to get some air, and he got a call from Luke, so Ryan answered the phone.

"Hello, Luke."

Luke said, "Hey, bud, what up?" Ryan was real slow on answering Luke back.

Then Luke knew there was something wrong and asked Ryan, "Hey, bud, what's wrong?" The only thing Ryan could said was repeating one word," Emily."

Luke said, "Bud, what about Emily?"

Ryan said, "Emily is in the hospital in a coma"

Luke said, " I will be there, in an hour, and we can talk."

"OK," said Ryan, and then he went back up to the ICU where Emily was. He sat there holding her hand and waited until Luke got there. Luke got to the hospital and went to the ICU and found Ryan. Luke and Ryan went down to the cafeteria and talked. Ryan told Luke everything that happened and told that he was going to stay as long as the nurse let him.

Luke said, "OK, bud. Let me know if anything changes."

Ryan said, "OK, bud, I will do that."

Luke left, and Ryan went back to the ICU to be with Emily. Ryan fall asleep holding Emily hand. That morning, Ryan told Emily why she in the coma.

"Emily, my love. You're a very special woman to me and I love you dearly. I'm here by your side as long as your parents are away." That afternoon, while Ryan was outside, he got a call on Emily's phone, and it was her parents. Ryan answered it, "Hello."

Her parents said, "Hi Ryan, where's Emily?"

Ryan took a minute to say something, and when he did, he

told them what happened to Emily.

Her parents said, "We are coming home. It will take a couple days."

Ryan said, "OK, I will see you then, and I am staying with Emily until you get here."

"OK, Ryan" With that, they both hung up the phone and Ryan went back up to the ICU. A couple days later, Ryan got a call from Emily's parents, and they were at the airport.

Ryan said, "OK, I will be there." Ryan left the hospital and went to pick Emily parents up at the airport. He got there in twenty minutes. Ryan put their bags in the car and helped Emily's parents in the car. After they left the airport. Ryan took Emily's parents to the coffee shop. They got to the coffee shop and went in. Emily's parents and Ryan got some coffee. Emily mom asked how her daughter was doing, and Ryan told her, "As from as I have seen, she is doing OK but I am not for sure, because the nurse won't tell me anything. Only you guys can find that out, because you're her parents."

They got done talking, and Ryan took Emily's parents to the hospital where Emily was. Emily's parents and Ryan got to the hospital and went to the ICU. Ryan pointed out the nurse that was watching over Emily and Emily's parents went to nurse and asked, "Hi there, we are Emily Luce's parents. How is our daughter doing?"

The nurse said, "Hi, Mr. and Mrs. Luce. I am Norma, her nurse, and your daughter is stable for the moment."

Emily's parents told Ryan, "We will take turn. You take the day, and I will take the night."

Ryan said, "OK, Mrs. Luce. We can do that."

This went on for about a month, and all of a sudden, about midnight, Emily opened her eyes and said, "Mom, is that you?"

Her mom said, with tears in her eyes, "Yes, baby, it me."

Then Emily asked, "Where's dad at?"

Her mom said to her, "He's at work, baby, and Ryan is going to come in the morning. I will call Ryan and tell him to bring dad by for you. Ryan and I been here by your side."

Emily said, "Thank you, Mom." With that, Emily's mom called Ryan that night to tell him that Emily came out of the coma and to pick up Mr. Luce in the morning around 8:00 A.M.

Ryan said, "OK, I will."

After Mrs. Luce got off the phone with Ryan, she called her husband and told him

"Emily is out of the coma. Ryan will be there to pick you up in the morning around 8:00 A.M. to bring you to the hospital."

He said, "OK, I will be ready when he gets here" That morning before he left to go pick up Mr. Luce, Ryan called Luke to tell he the news he got from Emily mom. Then he got into his truck and went to pick up Mr. Luce at his home. When Ryan got to Mr. Luce's house, Mr. Luce was waiting outside. He had gotten into Ryan's truck, and they both went to the hospital. When they got to the hospital, Ryan let him off by the door. Mr. Luce got out and went to the ICU while Ryan went and parked the truck. He then went up to where Emily was.

Emily said, "Hi, Daddy"

Her dad said, "Hi, dear, how are you feeling? Ryan will be up in a minute."

"OK, Daddy. I still hurt a little, but I'm doing better, the nurse said." When Ryan got to the room, Emily said to Ryan, "Hey Ryan, thank you, for staying with me while I was in the coma. I love you very much."

Ryan said, "You're welcome my love, and I love you too."

About three hours later, the nurse moved Emily to a room and said to the parents, "Emily will be able to go home in a week if, everything goes okay."

Emily's parents said, "OK." They went to tell Ryan and Emily what the nurse had said, and Ryan said to Emily and her parents, "After Emily gets out, I will take all you guys out to dinner if Emily up to it."

Emily said "Thanks, baby, and I love you." About a week later, Emily was released from the hospital, and Ryan came and picked Emily up from the hospital and took her home. Then, the next day, Emily, her parents, and Ryan went to dinner. They all went back to Emily house, and Emily and Ryan went to Emily's room and lay on her bed watching movies. While they were watching movies, Ryan was holding Emily the whole time, and when it got late, Ryan left and went home.

Chapter Eight

The Special Concert

 About a month after Emily came back home from the hospital, Ryan called Mr. Luce and asked, "Mr. Luce, may I marry your daughter?"

Mr. Luce said, "Yes, you may marry my daughter, and thanks for asking me." Then, Ryan was telling Mr. Luce his plans about asking Emily to marry him. Mr. Luce said, "I like that plan, Ryan, and I will go along with it."

The night that George Strait was playing, Ryan went to pick up Emily at her house, and Emily asked, "Ryan, where are we going tonight?"

Ryan said, "It's a surprise."

Ryan had Mr. Luce get there early to talk to the manager and George Strait about Ryan and Emily getting on stage, and the manager and George Strait said, "OK, we will play along with that plan. Just write that song down on paper when you guys are ready to do this."

Mr. Luce said, "OK,"

Then Mr. Luce went and texted Ryan to tell him, "Ryan, it's a go,"

Ryan said, "OK, and thanks, Mr. Luce." Emily and Ryan made it to the concert hall, and Emily's parents were waiting for them inside. They went into the place and found Emily's parents. They sat down, and all four of them ordered dinner and drinks. They all listened to the opening act, Reba McEntire. After they got done eating, George Strait came on stage singing, *Love Bug*, and Ryan and Emily went out and danced to the song.

While they were listening to George Strait songs, George Strait asked, "Does anyone one have a request?" Ryan wrote the song named, *Check Yes and No* on a paper and gave it to the waitress. The waitress gave it to George Strait, and he started playing the song. When he got done playing the song, he got on the microphone and asked, "Would Ryan and Emily please come up on stage?" Emily looked at Ryan in a confused look, and then they both walked up on stage. George Strait looked at Ryan and handed him the microphone and said, "Ryan, the stage is yours." And Emily had more of a confused look on her face.

Then Ryan looked at George Strait and said, "Thanks, George" And then Ryan dropped to one knee, in front of everyone, and looked up at Emily and said, "Emily Luce, would you marry me, my love?"

Before Emily could answer Ryan, she started crying happy tears and then said, "Yes, Ryan, I will marry you!"

After that everyone, started clapping and then George said to both Ryan and Emily, "I am happy for both of you guys, and I wish you all the best." Then, Ryan and Emily left the stage and went back to their seats. George Strait started singing, *I Cross My Heart.*

Emily looked at Ryan and said, "I love you, baby." For the rest of the night, Ryan and Emily drank and danced until the concert was over. Why Ryan was driving back to Emily's house, she told Ryan, "Baby, I had a really good time tonight and thank you for tonight." Then, they got to Emily's house, and Emily and Ryan went to the patio and talked for an hour. Ryan kissed Emily on the lips and told her bye and turned, and as he started to walk to his truck, Emily yelled Ryan's name. Ryan turned around, and then Emily asked, "Baby, would you like to stay with me tonight?"

Ryan said, "I would like to, but what would your parents say?"

Emily said, "My parents told me at the concert while you was in the restroom, that it's okay now if you want Ryan to stay the night."

Then Ryan said, "OK, my dear Emily, I will stay with you tonight." With that, Emily and Ryan went into the house and lay down and turned on the TV and the movie *War Room* was on, and as they lay there watching the movie and holding each other, they fell asleep. The next morning, Ryan woke up, and Emily was not in bed, so he got up to find her. She was in the kitchen, making breakfast for everyone.

When she saw, Ryan she said, "Hey baby, how did you sleep?"

Ryan said, "Wonderful, baby." "Baby, would you like to go and pick out your wedding ring today?"

Emily said, "Yes, baby, we can do that today."

Now breakfast was ready, and everyone sat at the table, and Emily's dad asked them both, "When is the wedding going to be?"

They both said, "It's going to be on December 10th."

Emily's dad said, "OK, and let me know if you guys need help with the wedding."

Emily and Ryan said, "Thanks, and if we need help, we will let you know." After breakfast, Ryan helped Emily clean up, and after they clean up, they went to the mall and looked at wedding rings. Emily saw this gorgeous ring that had eighteen diamonds in the shape of a cross in a sixteen karat gold band.

She told Ryan, "That is the ring I would like."

Ryan said, "OK, baby, when it is time, we can get that ring for you." After they left the mall, they went to Luke's house to tell him the good news. When they got to Luke's house, he was working on his truck. Ryan and Emily pulled up and Ryan yelled out the window and said, "Luke, how you doing bud?"

Luke said, "I'm doing well, and how are you guys doing?"

Emily said, "We have been well, and last night, Ryan proposed to me at the concert on stage!"

Luke told them both, "I'm really happy for you two!" Then Luke went into the house and brought out three beers. So they drank their beers. Then Ryan told Luke, "I need to get Emily home and I need to sleep."

"OK, bud, talk to you later." Ryan and Emily left Luke's house, and Ryan took Emily home and walked her to the door. Then Ryan went home, took a shower, got into bed and fell asleep.

Chapter Nine

Summer Camp

 The Sunday of June sixth, Ryan and Emily was in church and Sunday school class that they were in, was looking for some volunteers for the summer camp that the church kids go to. The teacher told everyone the camp will start on June twelve and it goes for two weeks and that the sign up sheet will be in the lobby. And the teacher asked if anyone wants to be a counselor for the camp. So Emily and Ryan talk it over and they both were off for that summer and thought it was a good idea to join the team has counselors. So they both went to the lobby of the church where

the sign up sheet was and read the flyer on the counselor job.

The flyer said: Wanted counselors! Duties involve Watching the kids, teaching the kids new things, the counselors having an easy positive attitude, and first aid and CPR training is a plus activities will be nature, swimming, wood carving for the older kids, building thing out of nothing, having fun at the camp, and many more things.

So Emily and Ryan signed up for the summer camp and thought they could have fun teaching young minds. When they got done, they went to hear the preacher's sermon in the main auditorium and when the preacher was done Emily told her father that Ryan and her sign up for the summer camp counselors. Emily dad said

"I'm happy for you, and it will be good for both of you guys, and it will give you guys, some time to hang out too."

When church was over, Ryan and Emily went to the store to get some things for one week of summer camp. They left the church parking lot and headed to Wal-Mart for the things they needed. When they got to Wal-Mart, they went for the personal stuff first, because Ryan needed some body wash, razors, toothpaste, and shaving cream. Emily had to get the same and some of the woman's personal things, too. After they found everything in the personal area, they went to the woman's clothing area, and Emily found a nice pair of shorts and a really cute shirt to go with the shorts.

She had to get a new pair of shoes, too. Then, they went to the men's clothing area and Ryan picked up some new pair of jeans and socks. Then, when they were done there, they went to the sporting goods area, because Ryan needed a new pocket knife, four canteens, and water tablets. They were done shopping for the things they needed and went to the checkout stand, they put all the stuff on the counter, and Ryan told Emily that he will pay for everything.

She said, "Thank you." Then she gave Ryan a kiss on the lips, and Ryan blushed a little bit. While the cashier was ringing up everything, she came across the outfits that Emily picked out and said, "These outfits will look good on you, girl."

"You know it will," said Emily.

When the cashier was done ringing up everything, the cashier said, "That will be one hundred nine dollars, and would it be cash or card?"

Ryan said, "It will be my card."

"Debit or credit," asked the cashier.

Ryan said, "Credit."

"Please slide your card," said the cashier, and Ryan slide his card and signed his name.

Then, the cashier said, "Here your receipt and thank you for shopping at Wal-Mart." Then, Ryan loaded up the cart and started towards the door.

The security guard asked Ryan, "Sir, do you have your receipt?"

"Yes, and here you go," said Ryan.

The security guard said, "Thank you, and have a good night."

"A good night to you too," said Ryan. Emily and Ryan walked to Ryan's truck to put the things inside. After the things were inside the truck, they got, in and Ryan took Emily home. When they got to her house, Ryan helped Emily get her stuff inside the house, and then Ryan left to go to his house to pack for the camp.

Two day before summer camp started for the kids, and Ryan went to pick up Emily, and they headed to the summer camp to get ready for the kids. The head counselor was there, along with all the other counselors. They had to listen to the head counselor give his speech on what is going to be going on for the next week, and that each day was going to be a different activity.There would be a list of activities by age group in the office.

Then, the head counselor asked a question, "Is there anyone that is First Aid and CPR trained?"

Two people stood up and said, "I am," and one of them was Ryan.

The head counselor said, "Good to have you guys on board," After the meeting, the head counselor took everyone to the office and got a copy of the lists for everyone. While they were waiting for their copies, they all read the list. The list said: "Ages from six to eight, learning about nature and animals, art and craft, singing, swimming, fishing. Ages from nine to thirteen: learning about nature, animals, tracking skills, nature walks, swimming, building things out of nothings, fishing, singing, and Ages from fourteen to eighteen: wood carving, swimming, archery, collecting firewood, and starting the fire for the night, tracking skills, fishing, and singing. After getting there, then the head counselor took them on a tour of the camp, and when that was over, everyone took their stuff to the cabins and went to the chow hall for some dinner.

When they got to the chow hall they smelled some really good food. The camp bought pizza for everyone for dinner, because the camp food wouldn't be there until the next morning. After dinner, Ryan and Emily took a walk and were holding hands around the camp before dark. When they got back, they went to their assigned cabins and fell asleep for the night, so they all can get up before the break of dawn. The next morning came around and they all heard the camp wake up tune. So they all got up, took their showers, and got dressed for the day.

The head counselor said to everyone, "Here are your duties for the day." Emily got cleaned up, and Ryan got to unloading of the truck and help others get stuff set up for when the kids got there the next day. Everyone helped each other until it was just time for bed.

The head counselor said, "Good job out there today and you all get a good night's sleep for tomorrow for when the kids get here, and they will be arriving around 8:00 A.M. in the morning. Good night and good luck, everyone!"

Everyone went to their cabins, so they could try to good night rest. At six o'clock in the morning of day one for the kids, everyone woke to wake-up music, so they all could get ready before the kids got there at 8:00 A.M. Everyone was up and ready, so they all went for chow. After chow, they all went to get the other list of what kids they had for the one week. It was now 8:00 A.M., and the buses were coming in, and there were about forty buses there. The counselors were collecting the kids and taking them to the cabins in which they would stay for the one week. After the counselors got the kids to the cabins and the kids got to unpack, the counselors went over the rules of the camp and the things that were going to happen in the next one week.

At about noon, the counselors took their kids to the chow hall and told the kids that they were going to go on a tour of the camp after chow. After everyone was done having lunch, the counselors took the kids on the tour, and all the kids were very excited. The tour of the camp took a good five hours, and then when the tour was over, it was dinner time. Everyone went to dinner and had hamburgers and mac and cheese with tea, juice, or water. When everyone was done, they all sat around the fire and, everyone introduced themselves. After that they all headed for the cabins to get a shower and get ready for bed. Some counselors that had the little kids read a book to them, before they all fell asleep.

At six o'clock in the morning of day one of summer camp, and everyone was just waking up. The counselors are now up getting the kids up for the day and getting them to the chow hall for some breakfast and they had made eggs, bacon, cheese sandwiches. After breakfast was done, everyone got into groups of what there age group is and waited to see what they were going to do that day.

The head counselor came up to the microphone and said there would be singing every night at the campfire and the ages six to eight and nine to thirteen children were going to be learning about nature and animals for day one, and two, three and four, art and crafts, and day five would be fishing and swimming.

The ages nine to thirteen children would be learning about nature and animals for day one and two. On day three would be a tracking skill on day four would be nature walks; on day five would be building something out of nothing. The age fourteen to eighteen would be doing a fire safety class on day one, and two would be a tracking skills class and collect wood for the campfire and the wood carving; on day three and four would be wood carving and singing. Day five will be archery.

On day six, everyone would be fishing and swimming. When the head counselor was done, the counselors got their kids and started to do the things with them. It was now noon, and everyone ran to the chow hall when they heard the bell. When lunch was over, everyone went back to doing what they were doing until dinner time came. It was now 5:00 P.M., and dinner time until 6:00 P.M. At six-thirty, they all got around the campfire, and at 8:00 P.M. was showers. Was 9:00 P.M. was light out, and this went on every day until the end of the week. On day seven, the counselors got the kids up and went for breakfast and got them ready for when the buses came to get them at around10:00 A.M. When the buses got there at ten o'clock in the morning, the counselors got the kids on the bus,

and the counselors had to stay two more days to help clean up the

camp before going home for the summer.

Chapter Ten

College Pride Event

Emily started college in January, because she needed a business class for her job. After a month in college, Emily was walking through the quad and saw a sign for a pride event.

The sign said, "Pride Rainbow Event with different vendors, giveaways, DJ, dancing and two shows on September 5th." She was thinking to herself that it would be fun for Ryan and her, and it was only was two days away, so she took a picture of the sign and sent it to Ryan with a message saying, "Hey, sweetie, would you like to go with me to this Pride Event here at the college? We still need to make a date for the engagement party!"

Ryan text back, "Sure, I would like to be more open-minded, and I can show you that dance I know. We can do the engagement party, and I will make all the arrangements."

"OK, dear, and what dance would that be?"

"You will see."

"OK, sweetie, and I love you so much. it means a lot to me how understanding you are."

"I love you too, baby-doll." He followed by that with a kiss and heart emoji. Then, Emily walked to her class. After class was over, she went home and went to her room. Once in her room, she put on the play list that Ryan made her with country, rock, soft pop, and love songs, while she was doing her homework. When her homework was done, it was so late at night, that she just crawled into bed and got her phone and sent a text to Ryan saying, "Hey dear, I just wanted to say good night, and "I love you." She stared at the picture of Ryan without his shirt on, showing all his muscles, until she fell asleep. Emily woke up to the phone going off, so she looked at the phone, and she saw a text from Ryan. She opened the text and it read:

"Morning, sweet heart. I hope you slept well, and I will come over after work. Let me know what you would like for dinner and what movie you would like to see tonight. I love you too,"

Emily text back with, "I would like sushi, and I am down with any movie you pick out, because I would be cuddled up to you and I may fall asleep next to you." Then, she went down to the kitchen and made some coffee to help her wake up before getting ready to go to the gym. Once she was ready, she left to go to the gym. She got to the gym and walked in.

A lady said to Emily, "Hey girl, how is it going?"

" It's going great, and how's the family?"

"Well, Cindy made it into the college she wanted, and my Mike just loves his middle school."

"Cool. What college she got into?"

"Sanford."

"Nice, and tell her I'm proud of her."

"I will, and I almost forgot, I'm two months pregnant."

"Congrats! Do you know where Tom is?"

"He is sick today, but he told me to send you over to Lisa today."

"OK," and with that Emily walked over to Lisa to get her exercises done. After two hours at the gym, Emily went home and hopped in the shower to clean up and put her hair up in curlers for the night. It was almost time for Ryan to get out of work, and she took out the curlers and put on a nice casual clothes and did her make-up. Then, her phone went off with a text from Ryan, "Hey, I'm on my way to your house now. See you when I get there and I heart you!" Emily got the blanket and put it on the couch and heard Ryan's truck pull up. Her heart started racing, and she took a quick look in the mirror to see if everything was good, and then she opened the door, took the food from Ryan, and let him in.

She said, "Go have a seat, and I will get the food dish out and join you." Ryan sat down in the living room and put the movie on the coffee table and relaxed on the couch. Emily came into the living room with the food and set it on the coffee table and sat next to Ryan and grabbed the movie.

She said, "*Wayne's World*" and handed it to Ryan to put it

in. Ryan took the video and put the movie into the DVD player. Then, he sat back down and got the controller and hit play. After they ate, Emily laid her head on Ryan's chest and cuddled up to him. Before the movie was over, she had fallen asleep, and when the movie was over, Ryan easily moved her head down on the pillow. He picked up their dishes off the coffee table, and took them into the kitchen, so he could wash them for her. Right before he left, he walked over and kissed her on the cheek and left something on the coffee table and went home.

When Emily woke up, she grabbed her cell phone and went to use the bathroom. While she was sitting on the toilet, she was looking at Face-book and replying to posts. After she was done, she went into the bedroom and started to look for something to wear to the pride event. She couldn't decide what to wear, so she called Cricket.

"Hey, Emily!"

"Hey girl, I need your help."

"What you need help with?"

"I have this Pride Event I'm going to, and I don't know what to wear,"

"I'm on my way over now."

"See you soon! Bye!" They hung up the phone. When Cricket got there, Emily let her in, and they when to her room. Once in the room, Cricket started looking at Emily's clothes.

Emily was saying, "You know, girl, you been a real supporter to me and the pride community, and one day I will find away to pay you back."

"Girl, you don't have to do that."

"I know I don't, but the truth is, if I didn't have you as a friend that cared about me and people like me, I don't know where I would have ended up, so thank you so much for being there for me."

"You're welcome, and here we go." Cricket pulled out a nice satin shirt with roses on it, followed by a nice pair of jeans, and Emily's Justin boots and laid them on the bed and said, "What you think?"

"I love it, and I totally forgot that I had that shirt in there."

"Well, what are you waiting for? Put them on, and let's see how you look!" Emily took off what she had on, in front of Cricket, and put on the clothes that were on the bed.

She asked, "Well, what you think?"

"Oh girl, with the right make-up on, you'll look really good!"

"You think so?"

"No, I don't think so, I know so, and where is that make-up of yours?"

"It's over there by my bed on the floor in a box." Cricket walked over to the box, picked it up and set it on the bed.

"Damn, Emily!"

"What?"

"You got lots of colors here. Come sit in the chair, and let me do your make-up." Emily walked over to the chair, and sat down, while Cricket did Emily's make-up. It took about thirty minutes but looked really good.

Emily looked in the mirror and said, "I love how you mix the rose-gold with the red eye shadow, and I love the cat-eyes too, because I have always liked them but couldn't ever get them just right."

"Thank you, Emily," and right then, the doorbell rang.

Emily walks to the door and said, "Who is it?"

"It's your sweetheart, Ryan." Emily opened the door and let Ryan in. Then, she introduced Ryan to Cricket.

Cricket said, "So, you're Ryan, I see!" and turned to Emily and said "well done" Emily started to blush and asked Cricket

"Are you going to come to the event with us"

"No, I have to get back home, because I'm streaming on *Twitch TV* tonight."

"Oh yeah, I forgot what day it was." So before Cricket left Emily's house, Emily gave her a hug, and Cricket left.

Ryan said, "Well, we should be going, too."

"Right." They left for the event. When they got there, it looked like the county fair. They parked and walked in and looked around.

Emily said, "Let's see what they have here."

"OK." The couple walked around for an hour, and Emily ran into a guy named Allen who people called Chezzy-nerd because he love eating cheese on everything, and he smart.

Emily ran up to Chezzy-nerd and give him a hug and said, "Chezzy, what are you doing here at a Pride Event?"

"Oh, hey there, Emily! I'm the DJ this year."

"Cool! They picked the right person, because on your streams, you DJ really well!"

"Thank you, Emily. You're one of my favorite viewers."

Emily blushed and said, "Chezzy, this is Ryan, the guy I told you I was dating."

"Nice to meet you, Ryan."

Ryan said, "Nice to meet you too. I watch you too!"

"Really? What is your name in the chat?"

Ryan said, "Bullrider23, but I don't talk much."

"Oh yeah, I remember you now. Sorry for cutting this short, but I have to get back to work. Emily, nice talking to yeah again!"

"Chezzy can you play my favorite song?" asked Emily.

"Sure. When you come by, I will."

"Thank you."

"Anytime! Bye!" Ryan and Emily said bye, too.

Then, Chezzy walked off and Emily turned to Ryan and said, "Let go see the fire show."

"OK." They walked over to where the fire show was. There was a lady with a fire baton, and she was spinning it while dancing. The lady did some normal dance moves, and all of a sudden, she did a back-flip with the fire baton. Emily cheered and was thinking she could just do a back-flip.

After that, Ryan said, "Sweetie, would you like to dance over by the DJ?"

"Sure, dear." They walked over to the dance floor and started to dance to the song playing.

Emily heard Chezzy say, "I have a special kind of person that is always in my streams, and this song is for you. Don't you ever change, Emily." Then, Chezzy put the song "Da Ba Dee" by Eiffel 65, and Emily started to blush.

She heared Ryan say, "It's your song! Go do your dance." She looked at him and didn't say anything but just jumped out there and danced. A few seconds later, Ryan and a lot of people jumped in and started to do the dance, too.

After the song was over, Emily said, "I didn't know you knew that dance."

"Remember the dance I wanted to show you?"

"Yes."

"That was it." Emily just kissed Ryan, and they went back

to dancing. After a while of dancing, Ryan and Emily walked over to the food area. When they got their, they looked at what was offered. They both saw the steak stand and walked over.

The lady said, "Can I help you two?"

"Yes, can I get two tacos with rice and beans?" said Emily

Ryan said, "Can I get a mid-rare rib-eye with chili?"

The lady yelled, "Two taco, rice, beans and a medium rare rib-eye, chili! That will be fourteen dollars." Ryan gave the lady the money. After about ten minutes, the food was done, and the lady called their names. Ryan went and got the food. Then Emily and Ryan sat down and ate. When they got done, they threw away the trash and walked over to the last show. The last show was the drag show, and Emily was having fun watching. Their was the Mad-hatter, T-Rex, and many others. When the show was over, Ryan and Emily walked back to the truck, and Ryan took Emily home.

When they got to Emily's house, Ryan walked Emily up to the door, and Emily kissed Ryan and told him, "I had a great time with you. Thanks for being understanding with everything."

Without saying a word, Ryan just gave Emily a long kiss

and told her, "I'll talk to you in the morning." While Ryan was

walking to his truck, Emily waved good-bye. Ryan drove off.

Then, Emily walked into the house and went to sleep.

Chapter Eleven

Engagement Party

The next morning, Ryan called Emily, and Emily answered, "Hello" in a very sleepy voice.

"Hey sweetie, did I wake you?"

"Yes."

"I'm sorry"

"It's okay. So what's up?"

"I got all the arrangements done, and the engagement will be a week from Saturday at The Roxy Noir."

"Nice, dear! How did you ever get a booking there?"

"I know a few friends that are managers/owners, and they

said that some people had canceled on them, and they had an opening."

"Cool, dear! I'll let you go for now, because I have to wake up some more, or I will fall back to sleep!"

"OK, sweetie. Take care!"

"You too, dear." They both said "bye" and hung up the phone. Emily fell back to sleep, after they got off the phone. Later that afternoon she called family and friends and invited them to a dinner on Saturday night, that next week. It would start at 6:00 P.M. and it would be on them. It will be held at The Roxy Noir. Then, she started working on a school presentation for her class.

Now, it was about two days from the party, and Emily didn't have anything nice to wear, so she called her friend River up.

"Hey girl, what up?"

"Nine-one-one, I have nothing to wear to the engagement party."

"Don't worry your party little head off. River here has got ya covered. We will see my friend Ash who owns The Mountain

Bridal Shop their in the mall."

"Cool! When can we go?"

"As soon as you get to my house, we can go!"

"OK, be their in ten minutes!"

"OK." They both said bye. Emily got ready, ran out of the house, and went to her friend River's house. When Emily pulled up to River's house, their was River watering the yard. When River saw Emily, they wave and said, "Let me turn this off, and grab my things, and then we can go."

"OK." Emily waited about five minutes and saw River come out of the house. River said, "Let go." They got into the car and went to The Mountain Bridal Shop. While they were headed there, a song came over the radio, and River said, " I need to turn this song up, because this is my jam."

After the song was over, River turned the radio back down, Emily asked, "That song was really good. What was the name of it?"

"Oh; *Dance,Dance* by Fall Out Boy. When I hear it, I can't help myself but turn that shit up."

They got to the mall parking lot and parked. They both

walked to The Mountain Bridal Shop to find a nice dinner dress.

When they got to the shop, a person came up and asked, "Hi there, my name is Sara, and welcome to The Mountain Bridal Shop, where we have the nicest dresses in the world. How may I help you two?"

River asked, "Is Ash here?"

"Oh yes, they are, and let me get Ash for you. Can I say who is asking?"

"Just tell Ash that River is here."

"OK!"

The sales lady left and went to Ash's office and knocked on the door and Ash said, "Yes, Sara?"

"There is person in front asking for you, and I think they said their name was River."

"Oh yeah, and tell them that I will be out there in about ten minutes."

Sara went back to the front and walked to River and said, "Ash said to give them ten minutes, and they would be out." Sara left and went back to work. After ten minutes, Ash walked out to greet River.

Ash said, "What brings you out this way?"

"Well, its my friend Emily, and she needs a dinner dress for her Saturday night engagement party"

"Umm, let me think here for a minute." Ash thought out loud and was saying, "Let see here. She's five-five, almost five-six, average size, and eyes are green. I got it. Please follow me." They followed Ash to a rack of really nice dinner dresses. Ash pulled a blue and a red dress off and hand them to Emily to try on, and Ash said, "The changing room is over their in the corner."

"OK," said Emily as she went to size them on.

About five minutes later, Emily came out in the red dress, and Ash and river said, "No, red is not you at all. Try on the blue dress."

"OK." Emily walked back into the changing room, and five minutes later, came back out in the blue dress.

Ash look at River and said, "What do you think"

"I like it!"

"Me too, Emily, what do you think about it?"

"I love it!" Emily went back into the changing room to take

off the dress and put her clothes back on and came back out.

Then she heard River say, "Girl you need some nice shoes too."

"You're right," so they walked over to the shoe part of the store.

River saw a nice pair of blue heels and asked Emily, "What you think about these?"

"Those would work." Emily got the shoes from River, and they walked up to the checkout counter, where Ash was waiting. Emily put the dress and shoes on the counter.

Ash rang everything up and said, "That would be one hundred and twenty dollars." Emily gave Ash her card. After Ash ran Emily's card, Ash said, "Thank you for shopping at The Mountain Bridal Shop. River, it's nice to see you again."

River said, "Its was nice seeing you again, too!" River and Emily left the mall and went back to River's house. Once they got their, Emily told River, "Thanks for helping me with picking things out for the party. If you like to come, you're more then welcome. It starts at six o'clock in the afternoon."

"You're welcome, and OK, thank you." They both said,

"bye," and Emily got into her car and went home.

Saturday afternoon arrived, and Emily was getting ready for the party. After all the prepping in the bathroom, she walked into her room and put her blue dress, then went back into the bathroom to put on her make-up and style her hair. She left the bathroom and put on her blue shoes on, and then the phone rang.

Emily pick up the phone and said, "Hey dear, what up?"

"Hey sweetie. Are you ready for tonight?"

"Yes I am, and when are you coming over?"

"I'm on my way over now."

" OK." They both hung up the phones, and Emily finished getting ready. Emily heard the knock on the door and when she looked to see who it was, it was Ryan, and she opened the door to let him in.

When Ryan stepped in the door, he said, "You look beautiful, in that blue dress," and Emily blushed, making her cheeks even redder.

She said, "Think you," in a happy-shy voice.

"Well, shall we get going to dinner? Because we don't want to be late for our own dinner party?" They both laugh about it, and then Emily said, "Let go." They walked out to the truck, and

Ryan opened the door for Emily, and Emily got into the truck.

Ryan shut the door and then went around and got into the truck

himself. They left for the dinner party. When they got to The

Roxy Noir, they saw that there was valet parking. Ryan pulled

up, and the valet guy opened the door for Emily.

Emily said, "Thank you, kind sir." and stepped out of the

car. Then the valet person went over to Ryan and gave Ryan a

ticket and parked Ryan's truck while Ryan and Emily walked

into the restaurant. Once in the restaurant, they both were greeted

by Jesus and Daniel the owners of the place.

Daniel said , "Hey Ryan, is this the lucky lady you told me

about?"

"Yes, this is, Emily. Emily, this is Daniel and Jesus, my

two oldest friends I told you about."

Emily said, "Hi there! It's nice to meet both of you!"

"It's nice to meet you too." said Daniel and Jesus, followed

by Jesus bringing Emily hand up and kissing the back of her

hand.

Emily just giggled and said, "Oh Jesus, how sweet you are,

greeting me with a French greeting, but I'm with Ryan." Then they laughed about it, because they knew Emily was joking around.

Jesus said, "please come with me, so I can seat you in your area." Emily and Ryan followed him to the area.

Then he said, "May I start you off with anything while you're waiting for your party to get here?"

"I would like a Dr Pepper," said Ryan.

Then Jesus said, "And for the lady"

Emily said, " I would like some blackberry punch."

Jesus walked away from the table to get the drinks for them.

About ten minutes later, Jesus came back with a few people and told Ryan, "If you need anything, Dan, Hannah, and Kate will be your servers."

"OK." Kate had the drinks, and Jesus walked off to take care of some things. After about fifteen minutes later, everyone started to show up and were seated in Ryan's area. Everyone was ordering their food, and twenty minutes later, everyone had their food and was eating.

Halfway through dinner, Ryan tapped his glass, and everyone looked up at Ryan, and said, "Emily and I invited all you guys to tell you all that we are engaged, and the wedding will be on December 10th." Everyone started clapping, and after everyone had finished eating, they talked for an hour before people started to leave. Right before Ryan and Emily left, they paid the seven hundred dollar bill and left three hundred dollars with Daniel to give one hundred dollars to each of the servers. Then Emily and Ryan left the restaurant and took Emily home before Ryan went to his house for the night

Chapter Twelve

Wedding Plans

Three months away from the wedding, Ryan and Emily called places to hold the wedding, and thank God, they had a call come in.

Emily answered the call and said, "Hello!"

The lady said, "Is this Emily?"

Emily said, "Well, yes it is. How may I help you?"

The lady said, "Well, Mrs. Emily, my name is Sue with the Wedding By the Sea Company, returning your call. We had a wedding cancel and wanted to see if you are still interested in booking your wedding?"

Emily said, "We will take it, and thank you!"

Sue said, "You're welcome. We will see you on December 10th."

They both said, "bye," and hung up the phone.

Ryan asked, "What was all that about on the phone?"

Emily said, "Baby, that was Wedding By the Sea, and we got the slot on December 10th."

Ryan said, "Cool, baby! Now we need to get everything else ready for that wedding!" With that Ryan and Luke went to the mall for tuxedos which took them about an hour to pick out. While they were at the mall they saw Emily there too with her mom.

Ryan asked, "what are you doing at the mall?"

Emily said, "Looking at wedding dresses."

Ryan said, "Cool, baby! I want your opinion on a tuxedo Luke and I picked out for the wedding."

"OK, honey."

With that, they all went to the tuxedo shop, and when Emily saw the tuxedo, she said, "I love it, baby. That would look good on you!"

Ryan said, "Thank you, honey, and I love you very much."

With that, Emily and her mom went one way, and Luke and Ryan went the other way. Ryan told Luke "Hey Luke, we need to go and get the wedding ring for Emily."

"OK, Ryan, and what kind of ring did you want to get her?"

"Well, Luke, I got Emily the eighteen carat gold ring with a one carat diamond on it and three crosses on the ring," Said Ryan

Luke said, "That's cool. How much are you getting it for?"

"Well, Luke, it costs me seven thousand dollars but my baby is worth every penny of it. The wedding is going to cost us twenty thousand dollars," said Ryan

Luke said, "Yeah, she is worth it, and she's like an angel from the heavens sent to you, Ryan." They got to the jewelry store to pick up the ring, and when they got there, they ran into an old friend that rode with Luke and Ryan in high school.

Luke and Ryan went up to James and said, "Hey, James, how have you been? Long time no see!"

"Hey guys, I have been well, and I'm married with two kids. How have you guys been?" asked James

Luke said, "I have been good, just been riding bulls, and Ryan and I went pro."

Then Ryan said, "I am good, about to get married myself. I'm here picking up the ring now."

"Who are you getting married to?" James asked.

Ryan said, "It's Emily."

James said, "The rodeo sweetheart?"

"Rodeo sweetheart?" asked Ryan

James said, "Yeah, I know Emily. I went to grade school with her and back then, she was a rodeo sweetheart before she hurt her leg and all. That's cool, guys, and she is an angel."

Thanks, man, and give me your address, and I'll send you an invitation to the wedding. "With that, James wrote his address down and gave it to Ryan with a phone number too. Ryan said bye to James and went and got the ring. After that, Luke and Ryan left the mall and went back to Luke's place to talk about the rodeo coming up at the end of December. About an hour at Luke's house, Ryan called Emily to see how she was doing.

Emily answered the phone and said, "Hey baby!"

"How's it going at the mall?" asked Ryan

Emily said, "Good! Mom and I found this pretty dress for the wedding."

"Cool, baby girl." Said Ryan

Emily asked Ryan, "Baby, I got to go, and can I see you in the morning to go over the list for the wedding and other plans for the wedding?"

"Yes, I'll see you in the morning, dear." said Ryan

Ryan turned to Luke and said, "I will catch you later, man. I got a long day tomorrow with Emily."

"OK, see ya, man!" Luke said. Then Ryan got into his car and went home and went to sleep. That next morning, Ryan's alarm went off at 7:00 A.M., and he got ready. Then he grabbed his key, and called Emily to see if she was up and ready, and she was. So Ryan left the house and headed to Emily's house to pick her up. When he got to her house, he got out and rung the doorbell, and Emily's mom answered the door and yelled for her and told Emily that Ryan was here.

Then Emily came up to Ryan and asked, "Are you ready to

go?"

"Yes, dear," Ryan said, and with that, they left Emily's house and went to the flower shop to order flowers for the wedding. After about three hours at the flower shop, they both picked out the flowers they wanted to be at the wedding.

They told the lady when and where the wedding was going to be, and the lady said, "OK. Your total will be three hundred dollars, and that is for making everything, delivering and setting the flowers up." Emily and Ryan paid the lady, and they left and went to another place to get catering for the wedding. They had gone to a place that one of Emily's friends told her about, that had the better food, so they went to Big Bubba House of Catering.

When they got to Big Bubba House of Catering, a guy walked up to them and said, "Welcome to Big Bubba House of Catering, where there is no party too small or to big. We cater them all. How many we help you today?"

Ryan said, "Well, sir, my lovely wife to be and I are going to be getting married on December 10th, and we need someone to cater for the wedding."

"Well, sir, you stopped at the right place. We have the best food that money can buy. So, what kind of food are you kids thinking about having for your wedding." asked the man.

Emily and Ryan said, "Well, we were thinking about beef and chicken."

"Those are a great choices, because it just so happens, we only buy the best meat in town from the local ranchers. All you have to do is let us know one week before the wedding on how many people are coming, and we will have everything ready," said the man. Then, both Emily and Ryan thanked the man and left the place and got into Ryan's truck and drove off. Emily asked Ryan if they should have a DJ or a band playing at the wedding.

Ryan asked, "if we have a band, who would you like it to be?"

Emily said, "We'll see, my first chore will be Blake Shelton, and my second one will be Miranda Lambert!"

With that Ryan told Emily, "Don't worry about that! I'll take care of that." They did all the running around, and Ryan took Emily out to a nice dinner and then went back to Emily home. They started making the list and made the invitations out. Emily would send them out in the morning. Two hours went by, and they were done, Ryan kissed Emily went home to his house. When Ryan got home, he made some phone calls to some of his friends about the music for the wedding, and most of his friends said to call Bob Cola, because he knew people.

Ryan called Bob Cola, who answered the phone, and said, "Hey, Ryan!"

"Hey Bob, I'm looking for a band or a DJ for the wedding, and people told me that you know people."

"I do, and what kind of music you looking for?"

"Well, it would be country music, and Emily would like to have Blake Shelton or Miranda Lambert, but she's OK with the DJ."

"OK, I will see what I can do for you, friend. Give me about a week or so, and I will call you back."

"OK." They hang up their phones. About six days later, Ryan's phone rang, and it was Bob, so he picked up.

"Hello, Bob."

"Hey, I got you a DJ for your wedding, but I have some

bad news."

"What's the bad?"

"One of my female friends came down with cancer, and I won't make it."

"It's OK, Bob. You go spend time with your friend, and you can see the pictures when you get back."

"Thank you, Ryan. I wish you the best!" They said their goodbyes, and hung up their phones. Ryan called Emily and told her that they had a DJ for their wedding.

Chapter Thirteen

Veterans Day

Emily called Ryan, and he picked up.

Emily asked Ryan, "Hey baby, what are you going to do for Veterans Day, today?"

Ryan said, "I was planning on going to the veteran's cemetery to see my grandfather and some friends that are buried there, then go to the homeless center to help out, and then off to go see the Veteran's Day Parade."

"I have a great grandfather there also," said Emily.

Ryan told her, "Be ready when I come by. I'll pick you up

in fifteen minutes."

"OK," said Emily. Ryan got ready and headed to Emily's house. In the mean time, Emily was getting ready, and she put on this beautiful sun dress with blue and red flowers and did her hair and makeup. Now, Ryan made it to Emily's house and was knocking on the door. Her dad answered and let Ryan in.

"So Ryan, how are you doing today?" asked Mr. Luce.

Ryan said, "I'm doing well, sir." At that time, Emily was coming down the stairs, and Ryan looked at her and said, "My dear, you sure look pretty today!"

"Why, thank you, Ryan," said Emily, and with that, she said bye to her parents and walked out the door. They both got in the truck and drove off. On the way to the cemetery, they stopped off for some flowers at the flower store, so they could put them on the graves at the cemetery. They got what they needed at the flower store and left. Before they got to the veterans cemetery, they saw a lots of American flags. They pulled in and parked. As Ryan was parking, he saw what looked like Bob's white truck in the parking lot. Then Ryan parked his truck and turned off the engine and they both got out. They both started to Emily's great grandfather's grave, and they both ran into Bob.

Ryan said to Bob, "Hey Bob, how you doing today? This is Emily, the little lady I'm going to marry."

Bob said, "Nice to meet you, Emily, and I'm doing OK. I'm just visiting my three buddies that I served with in World War II. What you two doing here?"

"Well, Emily's great grandfather, my grandfather, and two of my friends are buried here," said Ryan.

Bob said, "Cool." Then Emily noticed there were no flowers on the graves Bob was visiting, so she put some flowers on each grave.

Bob told Emily, "Thank you very much for putting some flowers on the graves."

"You're welcome, Bob. I wanted to thank you, too," Emily said.

"For what?" Bob asked in a confused sound.

"For running off the wolves, when you came out," Emily said.

"You're welcome! Ryan, I got to be going now," said Bob

Ryan said, "OK, Bob, we will see you around!" And with that, Bob left, and Emily and Ryan went to Emily's great grandfather's grave.

When they got there, Emily said to her great grandfather, "Hi, great grandfather. I want you to meet Ryan. He's the guy I'm going to marry. My parents are doing well, and I brought you some flowers." Then she put some flowers on the grave and turned to Ryan and kissed him. After that, they went to Ryan's grandfather's grave and put flowers on that and the same with Ryan's friends. After about an hour of being there, they walked to the truck and left the cemetery and headed to the homeless center to help out serving lunch. They got to the homeless center, packed and went in and got right to work. while they were there, Ryan came across an older man that knew Ryan's grandfather, and those two started talking. Ryan found out a lot more things about his grandfather. Then, Emily came by, and Ryan told Emily about him.

Ryan said to the man, "Oh sir, this is Emily Luce."

Then, man asked Emily, "Are you any relationship to John White?"

"Why, yes, sir. He is my great grandfather," said Emily.

Then the man said, "I knew both men, and I give high respect to them both." Now both Ryan and Emily had big confused looks on their faces. The old man explained how he knows them both.

"See, you two, Emily's great grandfather was my commanding officer, and Ryan's grandfather was my platoon sergeant during World War II. They both had respect for everyone and would give their lives to save everyone else. That's how your grandfather died, Ryan. He jumped on a grenade that the enemy threw into the place we all were in and saved everyone else. Your great grandfather died trying to save another man's life, who didn't see the sniper. They both will be heroes to me, because, Emily, I'm the one your great grandfather was trying to save out there."

Ryan told the man, "Thank you for the stories. We got to make the Veteran's Parade now. Bye!"

"Anytime, Ryan and Emily, and have fun at the parade." said the man, and with that, they left the homeless center and gotten in the truck and headed for the parade. Why they were driving to the parade, the traffic was a nightmare. They moved up real slow, and about thirty minutes later in traffic, they made it to where someone had hit a telephone pole. There were a lot of cops directing traffic and two fire trucks trying to get the person out of the car. Ryan and Emily got to where the parade was just in time before the parade started. They parked the truck and walk up to the parade. The parade has started, and they saw all branches of the military there, with the color guards and some of their vehicles. After all the vehicles passed the Air Force were the last ones to go by, and right at the end of the parade, the Air Force planes flew by and gave a little show. Then, the parade was over, and Ryan and Emily walked back to the truck and got in. Ryan started the engine and drove off.

"Hey baby," Emily said

Ryan answered, "Yes, beautiful?"

Emily said, "I had a very good day today, meeting that man today at the homeless center. I feel closer to my great grandfather, and I truly love you, baby."

"I agree with you about everything, and I love you too, beautiful," said Ryan. After that, they listened to the radio station called K-LOVE on the way to Emily's house. Ryan got out of his truck and went to the passenger door and opened it for Emily. Then he walked Emily up to the door of her home. Before he turned to leave, he kissed Emily and told her good night. Then, he walked to his truck, and she said bye and went in the house. Now, at his truck, he got in and drove home.

Chapter Fourteen

The Hunting Trip

&

Thanksgiving

 Ryan took Luke and Mr. Luce to Bob's house one afternoon to talk to him about coming over for Thanksgiving dinner, since Bob didn't have any family in town.

Bob answered, "Well that's kind of you guys to invite me to Thanksgiving dinner, but I won't feel right if I didn't bring something."

Mr. Luce said, "What would you like to bring?"

"Well, we all can go on a hunting trip to get some meat," said Bob

They all said, "What a good idea!" So it took about a week to get things together for a five day, hunting trip. About a week later, they all met at Bob's house, and they packed Bob's truck and took off for Hunter Peak Mountains. As they were on their way to Hunter Peak Mountains, they saw this store and a small restaurant, and since they were getting hungry. They stopped and went to the restaurant to get burgers and fries. When they got done eating, they went to the store. Ryan found this beautiful necklace that looked like a heart that had pretty Opals in it. It was a hundred dollars, so Ryan bought it for his baby doll back home.

He heard Bob said, "Let's go," so they all loaded up into the truck and resumed the drive to Hunter Peak Mountain. When they got to Hunter Peak Mountain, they saw lots of animals there. There were pheasants, deer, and ducks.

Bob said, "We're here for some pheasants, ducks and turkeys." They started to unpack the truck. After unpacking the truck, they started putting up camp for the five days. While the guys were making camp, Bob made dinner. Now camp was up, and they heard Bob say, "Dinner's ready!" They all started eating. While they were eating, everyone was telling stories about their lives. After they got done eating, they all cleaned up, and everyone hit the hay for the night. On day two, about 3:00 A.M., in the morning, the temperature got real cold and felt like thirty degrees. Bob got up and was making breakfast and started the coffee. About 3:30 A.M., the coffee was ready, and the others were waking up to the smell of the food and the coffee. Breakfast was ready, and they all got some breakfast. After breakfast, they went fishing and hiked up to the creek, where there were lots of trout.

Ryan said, "Dang, Bob, there are some real big trout in here!"

"Well, Ryan, my grandfather took me here when I was eight years old to fish and hunt, and I had a bust," said Bob. They all started to rig their fishing poles up and throw them into the creek. An hour went by, and Luke was watching his pole. All of a sudden Luke's pole started to go wild with a fish that jumped on his line, and Luke jumped up and set his line, hooking the fish.

Luke said, "I think I have a big one!" So the battle was on, fighting the fish onto the bank. After thirty minutes of fighting the fish, the fish jumped in the air, and all there eyes lit up. The trout looked like it could be about three feet long, and after about ten minutes, the fish jumped and the line broke on Luke's pole. Luke was really mad, because that trout would have been a nice one to hang on his wall. Then, it was an hour after Luke's line broke, and Ryan and Bob's poles started going off. They ran to their poles and started battling their fish. They both battled their fish for twenty minutes, and when they landed their fish, come to find out, there was just one fish, and Ryan hooked the mouth, and Bob hooked the side of the tail of a rainbow trout that was two foot eight inches. About two hours later, fish were biting like crazy, and they ended up with five rainbow trout and five brown trout. Later that afternoon around 7:00 P.M., the fish stopped biting, and they packed up and started back to camp.

When they got back to camp, Ryan said to Bob, "Hey, Bob, I will give you a break on cooking, and I will cook up the fish."

"Thank you, Ryan," said Bob. Then about forty-five

minutes later, the fish was done, and they all started to eat. After

dinner, it was 10:00 A.M., and they all went to bed. The morning

of the third day , they all slept in until about 7:00 A.M., and the

weather was warmer than the day before. Mr. Luce was making

coffee and why it was making the others started to wake up to the

aroma of the coffee. When everyone was up and moving around,

the coffee was done.

When the coffee was ready, Mr. Lace said, "The coffee

ready." Everyone poured themselves a cup of coffee and started

packing for the hike that day. When everything was ready, they

stood around talking about what was out in those woods.

Luke asked Bob, "What is the real danger out in those

woods?"

Bob answered Luke, "Well, Luke, there are mountain lions,

bears, snakes, bobcats, and wolves out there."

Luke looked at him and said, "Well, I'm taking my rifle

with me."

Bob said, "That's a good idea, and we all should do that too

and bring our knifes, too." All of them were now ready for the

hike with their packs on their backs, their rifles in their hands, and their knives on their sides.

Then Bob said, "Let go!" Everyone started on the hike. While on the hiking trail Ryan saw a family of deer. Near the trail, there was a doe, fawn, and a buck that had a good looking rack on it that looks like the buck had fourteen points on his rack.

Ryan turns and said, "Look, everyone!" Everyone stopped and looked. Luke pulled out his camera and took a picture of the family of deer. After about ten minutes, they started hiking again. The time was about noon, so they stopped to eat an MRE. While they were eating, they saw some raccoons playing off in the distance and the birds singing in the trees. Thirty minutes had passed, and they finished lunch and started hiking again. After hiking for another hour, they came to a waterfall with a small river. The river had good vegetation around it.

Ryan asked Bob, "What about this spot?"

Bob answered, "You know, Ryan? This spot would be good." Just then, they saw some turkeys, ring neck pheasants running on the ground, and ducks flying by. When the guys found their spot to hunt, they turned and started heading back to camp. Why they were on the trail, Bob was putting up ribbon, so they can find a spot in the morning. When they were almost to camp, Ryan heard what sounded like a rattle a little way up. Everyone stopped.

Bob said, "Everyone stay here, and I will go and check it out." After about ten minutes, the guys heard the rifle go off. Then, Bob came back with a five foot timber rattler in his hands.

Bob told Ryan, "It's a good thing you heard that snake, or one of us would have died." When they got back to camp, Bob started cleaning the snake and then cooked it up for dinner. When the snake was done, Bob called everyone, and everyone got a piece of snake.

While they were eating, Luke asked Bob, "Where did you learn how to cook snakes?"

Bob said, "When my grandfather and I came out here, he taught me how and what we ate out here while we hunted."

Luke looked at Bob and said, "It's good." Everyone said something. After dinner was over, everyone went to bed to get some good rest for the hunt in the morning. The morning of the day four, Luke woke up around 2:00 A.M., and he was so excited, like a kid in a candy store. While Luke was up, he was making coffee, and when it was about dawn, everybody else with that fresh morning air.

Ryan looked at Luke and said, "Well, someone got up early today, and I think it rained a little last night."

Luke said, "I know, but it sure smells good, and I couldn't sleep, because I'm too excited."

"Everyone is excited to go hunting, silly," said Ryan, and then Luke started laughing.

Bob said, "We have to start hiking to get there before the animals do, and we can get set up." With that, they started hiking to the spot they found yesterday. After two hours hiking, they made it to their spot and started to set up, and after they got set up, they sat and waited for the animals to come to them. At around 8:00 A.M., a flock of mallard ducks was flying by, and the guys aimed and fired their guns. They had gotten three mallards, that dropped from the sky, and Ryan went to get them. Everyone started packing their stuff up. When Ryan returned with the ducks, he packed his stuff, and they walked up a little way from where they were and saw some turkeys off in the distance. Bob stop everyone and looked on how many turkeys were over there. There were about ten turkeys.

Bob said, "Ryan and Mr. Luce, I want you two to come with me, and Luke, I want you to man the call and call the turkeys in to us." While Luke went to get the call and got into position, Mr. Luce, Bob, and Ryan were in their positions. Then, Bob waved his hand to Luke, and Luke started calling the turkeys in to them with an turkey call.

"It was working, three turkeys were coming into where we are by that new turkey call, Luke got," said Ryan. The others aimed and when the turkeys were close enough that the three guys fired their guns. The three turkeys dropped, and the men went out to get them. The other seven turkeys ran away after hearing the gunshots. Now the time was about 4:00 P.M. in the afternoon and started hiking back to camp. Half way back to camp, they came to a pond into which the river flowed, and there was some pheasants there. Luke told the others to stop. He aimed with his rifle and took the shot. Everyone's eyes lit up, because when Luke took the shot, he hit two pheasants at the same time!

Everyone told Luke what a good job he did. They picked up the pheasants and headed for camp. When they got back to camp Bob, Ryan and Luke were cleaning all the birds they got that day, and Mr. Luce went for ice at thirty minutes away. When Bob, Ryan, and Luke got done cleaning the birds, they took one of pheasants and started cooking it for dinner that night. When Mr. Luce got back, the pheasant was ready, and Mr. Luce put the ice in the ice chest with the three ducks, three turkeys, and one pheasant. Then, Mr. Luce went and got a piece of the pheasant. When they were eating, the men were talking about the day and when they were all done with dinner.

They cleaned up and went to bed for the night. The morning of the last day of the hunting trip came, and everyone slept in and didn't wake up until 9:00 A.M. They are all moving slow, because they had been going hard for four days straight. While one was making the coffee, the others were helping make breakfast. About thirty minutes later, the coffee and breakfast were done, and they all sat down to eat. Then, when everyone was done, they all started cleaning up, taking down their camp, and parking the truck to get ready for the drive home. It's now noon time, and they have a long drive home. So, at 12:30 P.M., they left the camp and started driving home. On the way home, they stopped at the store to get some more ice for the meat they got on the hunting trip.

Bob said, when at the store, "We need to get a room for the night, because a storm is coming in."

Everyone said, "OK, Bob." They all got a room for the night. Everyone was asleep except Ryan because he was thinking about Emily and how he missed her very much. Ryan looked at the heart necklace that he had gotten her and that would be a Christmas gift. Ryan fell asleep around midnight, and then, that next morning, when everyone woke up around 7:00 A.M., they came out of their rooms to find a tree that had been up rooted by the storm that happened the night before. They thought to themselves, "Let's get some food." So they all went to the little diner and had some food. Then, after they ate, they went back to their rooms and got their stuff and loaded it in the truck, and Bob got some ice to put on the meat. Then they left for home. At about noon, they made it back to Bob's house, and everyone got out of the truck and started unpacking the truck. When the guys were unpacking, Bob took the meat and put it in a bag with salt water.

Ryan came in the house, and asked Bob, "Why he put salt water in the bag with the meat."

Bob said, "It takes the game taste out of it." Ryan helped Bob put the meat in the freezer. Then, when that was done, they both went back to help the other guys out putting the things in their trucks.

After that, they told Bob, "We had a great time hunting and we all have to do this again sometime."

Bob said, "You're all welcome, and we should do it again, because I haven't felt this way in years." Everyone said their goodbyes and went home.

About a week later, it was Thanksgiving, and Ryan, Emily, Luke, and Bob went to Mr. and Mrs. Luce's house for Thanksgiving. When Ryan, Emily and Luke got to the house, they had a duck, and fifteen minutes later, Bob showed up and he had the turkey. They both gave the ducks and turkeys to Mrs. Luce, and she prepared them and put them in the oven. While the men were in the living room watching football and talking, Mrs. Luce and Emily were in the kitchen, cooking and getting things ready for the dinner. When the women were done, they joined the man in watching the football game. After about six hours later, dinner was ready and everyone was around the table eating and talking about the past and laughing about the crazy things that happened in their lives.

When dinner was over, the men said, "Since you made dinner, we can clean it up, and you women can go rest." With that, the women kissed their husbands and went and sat in the living room and knitted and talked about stuff. After the men got done cleaning the kitchen and putting the food away, it was 8:00 P.M., at night, and everyone left and went home for the night.

Chapter Fifteen

The Wedding Day

 December *10th* arrived, and Emily woke up a little nervous and happy about the day, since it's was the day she would be getting married to the man she loved. As she was getting ready in the morning, she noticed something on the nightstand; it was a note.

It read:

"Dear my love,

I knew you would need something old, and I would be honored if you could wear the object in the box, since it is something special to me. You are special to me in my heart.

Love you, my love,

Ryan"

With that, she opened the box and found a locket with a rose in the middle made from diamonds. When she took it out of the box and opened the locket, she saw a picture of herself and Ryan on their first date. On the other side of the locket, there was this message:

"To my love

I will always love you from the bottom of my heart from now and until we meet again.

Love,

Ted"

After she read that, she thought about it and said to herself, "Wait, Ted was Ryan's great grandpa, and this locket must be his great grandma's."

As she put the locket on, her heart started to beat a little faster, and her face glowed as it filled up with more love for Ryan. She finished getting ready and headed to the place where they were going to get married. Emily arrived and started to cry because of how beautiful the outside of the place looked. There were lots of red, blue, white, purple roses where Ryan and Emily would be standing. There were carnations at each end of every bench seat, all the colors all the round the area, and an overview of the sea. When Emily walked in, she saw the reception place where they would go after the ceremony and it just looked so beautiful. Then, Emily went into the room where she would get ready for the wedding.

Ruth said to Emily, "Girl, Why are you crying?"

"I'm crying, because everything is so beautiful, and it's everything I pictured it would be."

"I see what you mean, and you know, your a lucky girl to have a nice, good-looking man that loves you a lot."

"I know, and he left me a locket to wear, and it was his great grandma's."

"That was sweet of him to do that, but, girl, if you don't want to be late for your own wedding, we need to start getting you ready."

Ruth, Marlene, and Victoria were Emily's bridesmaids. Ruth started doing Emily's hair, and it took her two hours, because Emily's hair went past her derriere. Ruth did this lovely braid with a flower made out of a part of Emily's hair. Victoria started on Emily's makeup. She put on some foundation and started putting on some rose-gold eyeshadow with a lighter color and mixed them together, followed by the smoky charcoal eyeliner and mascara to make Emily's eye stand out. Then, Victoria put some blush on Emily's cheeks and a little highlight around the cheeks and jawbone. They applied some lipstick that matched Emily skin tone. The whole time Victoria was doing the makeup, Emily's eye color kept changing with each color that Victoria was putting on her. With Ruth doing the hair, Victoria was doing the makeup, and Marlene was doing Emily's nails and put a light rose color that match the eye shadow.

All three ladies said, "Girlll, I cant believe just how beautiful you are!"

"Now, you already have something old, and you need something borrowed, something new, and something blue. so you can borrow my head piece that has blue opals in it" said Ruth.

"Now you need something new. I wanted to wait, but here is the bracelet I picked up for you," said Marlene.

"Now for the something blue" said Victoria as handed Emily a pair of earrings

"Thank you so much for everything. If you three weren't by my side all these years, who knows where I would be. You guys are the best, and I love you guys," said Emily.

Ruth went to check to see if it was time for Emily to walk down the aisle. When Ruth came back, she told Emily, "Well, I hope you are ready, because they're ready for you."

"I am so nervous right now."

"All is going to be OK. You got this, girl!"

So all four of them went to the door, waiting to go in. Ruth gave the signal to the person that would start the wedding. The music started playing, and Ruth was watching for the signal to start coming down the aisle. After about fifteen minutes later, the music started playing, and the person gave the signal, and Ruth told Emily, "It's time."

Ruth sent the flower girl down the aisle. Marlene and Victoria were next to go down. Then, Ruth went after them. Emily took a deep breath and walked through the door. She saw everyone there and said to herself, "I want to cry, but I can't mess up my makeup." Then, she walked down the aisle very slowly with her dad.

When they got to the end, the preacher asked, "Who here gives Emily away?"

"My wife and I do," said Emily's step dad.

Then he handed Emily off to Ryan, and the preacher started saying, "Dear family and friends, we are gathered here today to bear witness and celebrate Ryan and Emily in marriage. They know each other and are understanding each other. They have grown and matured and decided to tie the knot and live as a husband and wife. I heard you two want to say something to each other."

"Ryan, when I met you that day at the rodeo, I knew I needed to know you. The day I fell in love with you was the day we were watching the stars, and you were so sweet, and I knew then I wanted to spend our life together," said Emily.

"Emily, I know it took me a little time to ask you out, because I was a little shy, but the day I met you, I knew I found the lady of my dreams," said Ryan.

"Do you, Ryan, take Emily to be your wife, to have and to

hold from this day forward, for better or for worse, for richer or poorer, in sickness and in health, to love and cherish, from this day forward until death do us part?"

"I do," said Ryan,

"Do you, Emily, take Ryan to be your husband, to have and to hold from this day forward, for better or for worse, for richer or poorer, in sickness and in health, to love and cherish, from this day forward until death do us part?"

"I do," said Emily.

"The rings, please".

Ruth handed the ring to Emily, and Luke handed Ryan the ring.

The preacher told Ryan, "Repeat after me."

"With this ring, I thee wed." Ryan repeated and put the ring on Emily's finger.

"Emily, repeat after me, with this ring, I thee wed." Emily repeated and put the ring on Ryan's finger.

"With the power invested in me, I pronounce you husband and wife, and you may kiss the bride."

Ryan leaned in and kissed Emily. Everyone stood up,

clapping. Then, the music started playing while Ryan and Emily walked down the aisle, through the doors.

Everyone met in the reception place to cut the cake, have dinner, and the two dances, then the party and pictures. They took the pictures. When everyone was seated the food came out and was served to everyone. The bride and groom made a toast and were thanking everyone for coming to their wedding.

Then they said, "Let's eat."

After about an hour, Emily and Ryan opened the gifts and cut the cake. Ryan wasn't expecting what Emily did. Emily put the cake into Ryan's face and then started gigging about it, so Ryan did it back to her. They were both laughing about it. Then, after they got cleaned up. Ryan said it was time for the father and daughter dance. The DJ started playing called, *Father and Daughter* by Paul Simon that Emily had picked out, because it was their song.

Then, after they were done, the groom and his mother danced to this song called, *Forever Young* by Rod Stewart.

The DJ said, "Will the bride and groom please come to the dance floor?" When Emily and Ryan got in the middle of the dance floor, the DJ stepped back quietly, and some people started playing the song, *It's Your Love* and all of the sudden, Emily heard Blake Shelton start singing, While they were dancing.

Ryan knew how much he loved her just by looking into Emily's eyes. Then, Emily heard Miranda Lambert start to sing, her part in the song, and at the end, Ryan noticed that Emily had tears coming out of her eyes, and he didn't say a thing but held her in a tight hug and knew she loves him, too. When the song was over, Emily makeup was running, and Ryan just pulled out his handkerchief and wiped Emily's face.

After he was done, Emily just pulled him into her and gave Ryan a big kiss and said, "I love you so much!"

Then Ryan said, "I love you, too, sweetheart," and kissed her back.

The DJ came back on stage and said, "Let's thank Blake Shelton and Miranda Lambert for being here. Emily and Ryan, this was a Gift from Bob Cola. Blake and Miranda joined in the party and gave Emily a signed picture of both Miranda and Blake and took some pictures with Emily. Then the DJ said, "Now, shall we get this party started?" and everyone yelled, "Yeah!"

The DJ kicked the music up, and everyone started dancing.

About three hour later, everyone was leaving and going home. Emily's father handed Ryan an envelope and said, "Wait until you get home to open it."

When they got home, Ryan opened the envelope, and it was a five days and four nights trip to Hawaii in January.

Chapter Sixteen

Christmas

It was now December and Emily and Ryan were in their house in Caney City, Texas. They were sitting there, thinking about what they could do for people that Christmas. The next morning, they went to the park, because it was a nice sunny day, and they went for a walk. They went to a small diner for lunch, and there was a Christmas tree with some small envelopes on it.

Ryan asked the lady, "What are the envelopes were use for?"

The lady said, "It was for the local orphanage, and that

they, hung up the envelopes, to try and help the kids out."

Ryan said, "Thank you," and walk over to the tree and took five of the envelopes, then went back to his seat. When the lady came back to take the order, she noticed that Ryan had picked up five of the envelopes.

She said, "Thank you," to Ryan for doing that, because most people just walked by it. She then took their order. When she was done, Emily and Ryan opened the envelopes. They started to read them.

The first one read, "My name is Cassandra, and I'm 8 years old. What I'd like for Christmas is a doll to play with. The second one read, "My name is Tom. I'm seven years old, and I would like a new pair of shoes, size six." The third one read, "My name is James. I'm ten years old, and I would like something to draw with." The fourth one read, "My name is Kasmia. I'm twelve years old, and I would like a paint kit." The fifth one read, "My name is Emma. I'm five years old, and I would like a family," and that last one broke Emily's heart to hear. When their food came, Emily put the envelopes in her pocketbook.

While they were eating, they were talking about what else they could do to help. Ryan was thinking and had a thought, "What if we did a raffle at the Christmas party in two weeks at the house?"

Emily said, "That's a good idea, and we can sell tickets for twenty dollars each and donate the money to St Jude's Children's Research Hospital. We also can get stuff animals and give them to the kids here in one of the local hospitals. Then, we can go to the shelter and hand out food.

Ryan said, "Sounds good, and I love you so much."

Now, they were done with their lunch and left for the mall to pick up some of the things listed on the envelopes before they went home. They arrived at the mall, and like always, the mall was packed and it was hard to find parking.

So Ryan dropped off Emily at the front while he found a parking space. Emily went to Starbucks and was waiting in line to order. When she got up to the front, The cashier asked, "What would you like?"

Emily told the lady, "I would like to have Venti Caramel Macchiato and a Venti Green Tea please, and Emily paid.

When the drinks were ready, Ryan came up to Emily and said, "Thank you, dear." Then they went to the shoe store first. They went in the shoe store and looked around for thirty minutes. They found an awesome pair of shoes. The shoes had superman on them, and they lit up. They paid for the shoes and went to the toy store for a doll. They got to the toy store, and there in the window was a doll that came with a lot of stuff, so they talked it over, and then, they picked up some markers, colored pencils, paint and a canvas.

When they got up to the cashier, to check out, they told him they would like the doll in the window and everything that came with it, so the man went and got it. They paid for everything and left.

As they walked through the mall, Ryan asked, "Emily would you like to go by the stuffed animals store?"

Emily said, "Yeah lets, go we can pick up some of them for the kids at the hospital." So they went to *Build a Bear* store and bought around one hundred and fifty bears for the kids. Now, it was getting late, so they decided it was time to go.

They headed for their car and put everything in the car and

headed home for the night. When they got home, Ryan carried all the stuff into the house. Then, Ryan went into the kitchen to make dinner while Emily put the stuff away and picked out a movie. After the stuff was put up, Emily came into the kitchen to see what Ryan was making homemade fried chicken, mashed potatoes, fried okra and brown gravy. She gave him a kiss and went to check her emails before dinner. When dinner was ready, Ryan told Emily, so while Ryan was putting the food on the plates, Emily was getting the movie ready for them .

The movie was called, *Kiss and Cry,* and Ryan brought the plates into the living room and set them on the coffee table, then went to turn the lights down low while they watched the movie and ate. Emily hit play on the movie, and when they were done eating. Emily curled up to Ryan with a blanket to watch the rest of the movie. When the movie was over, they both went into the kitchen and started to clean up. When that was done, they both went to the bedroom and got into bed, kissed each other, and Ryan put his arm around Emily, and they both fell asleep.

Over the next two weeks, Emily and Ryan had important business to take care of before they went to the hospital: the party at their house and the orphanage. When all that was done, they both went to Best Buy to pick up some prizes for the party in the next few days. After they got the prizes, they went home and got the house ready for the party, then went to bed. Now the morning of the party arrived, and Emily and Ryan cooked all day for the party that going to happen that night. They made cakes, pies, and appetizers. About one hour before the party was going to start, their guests started to show up, so the party started early. They started to sell raffle tickets to all the guests and everyone was having fun.

It had been two hours and Ryan got on the microphone and said, "Thanks to everyone that has came out and helped raise money for the St. Jude's Children's Research Hospital. It's time for the raffle, and we have three gifts to giveaway. The first item is a Vizio Smart-Cast, 38 inch, five point, one channel, sound bar system with sub-woofer." Emily drew the winning ticket, 390, and Mr. and Mrs. McCoy went up to get their prize.

The second one was a Sony Play-Station 4 Pro console with a gift card of fifty dollars, and Emily drew the ticket, and the ticket number was 566. Mr. and Mrs. Sanderson went up and got their prize. Now, the grand prize was a MSI 18 inch laptop with an Intel Core I-7, 64 gigabyte of memory, 2x NVidia Geforce GTX 1080, 1 terabyte hard drive with one terabytes solid state drive. Emily drew the ticket, and the ticket number was 229. Mr. and Mrs. Templeton went up to get their prize.

Ryan and Emily both said, "Thank you, again for helping out and for being here. We raised ten thousand dollars for St. Jude's Children's Research Hospital." Everyone started to clapping and the party started back up until ten o'clock came around, and everyone started to leave. After everyone was gone, Ryan and Emily cleaned up after the party and headed to bed. Now, it was three day before Christmas, and Emily and Ryan loaded up the stuff for the orphanage into the car and drove over there. When they showed up at the orphanage, Sister Kelly was waiting for them, and she helped Emily and Ryan carry in the stuff for the kids. When they handed out all the gifts, everyone but Emma was happy. While Ryan was talking to the Mother Teresa of the orphanage, Emily went over to talk to Emma.

"Hey there, Emma! What's wrong?

Emma said, "Everyone got what they asked for but me."

Emily said, "Cheer up! I think Santa Claus gave your gift to Mother Teresa, Why don't you ask her when Ryan comes out from talking to her?

"OK, I will," said Emma.

When Emma saw Ryan and Mother Teresa come out of the room, Emma asked Mother Teresa, "If Santa Claus left her gift with her?"

Mother Teresa said, "Santa Claus did leave your gift with me, Emma. Would you like to see it?"

"Yeah, where is it?

"OK, Emma, close your eyes," Mother Teresa said, and Emma did, and a few minutes later, Mother Teresa said, "OK, you can open them," and Emma looked around but didn't see anything.

She asked Mother Teresa, "Where is it?

Mother Teresa said to Emma, "Ryan and Emily are your new mommy and daddy." Emma had tears in her eyes and a bright smile on her face, and they let Emma play with the kids while Mother Teresa collected Emma's things and gave them to Ryan, and he put them in the car. After an hour, Emily, Emma, and Ryan got into the car and drove home. When they got home, Emily took Emma to her new room while Ryan carried in Emma stuff and sat them in her room.

"Emma, would you like to watch a movie, while we get dinner ready?" asked Emily.

Emma said, Yes, please," Then Emily brought up Netflix, and Emma picked out the movie called *Mulan II*. Emma sat in the chair watching the movie while Emily and Ryan made dinner, and when dinner was made, Emily went to pause the movie.

She told Emma dinner was ready, and they sat around the table eating and getting to know each other. When dinner was over, Emily took Emma for a bath and to get her new pj's on while Ryan was cleaning the kitchen. After everything was done, they all three sat on the couch to watch the rest of *Mulan II*. After that movie was over, Emily took Emma to bed, and Emily read Emma a bedtime story. When Emma was asleep, Emily went to the bedroom where Ryan was and curled up next to him and kissed him and said, "I love you so much" then fell asleep.

On Christmas morning, they all three woke up, had

breakfast, and got ready to go to the hospital. While Emily was getting Emma ready to go, Ryan got all the stuffed animals and put them in the car. Ryan was in the car, warming it up, when Emily and Emma came out and got in, and they went to the hospital. Now they were at the hospital, and Ryan dropped them both off at the door, so he could park the car, then walked back to them. They went into the hospital and talked to the higher up, and he came down to them to take the three of them to where the kids were. After about ten minutes, they went to were the kids are, and Ryan was talking to the man while Emily and Emma were passing out the stuffed bears to all the kids.

That took over an hour to pass them out, and then, the three of them left the hospital and went to Emily's house to let Emma see her new grandparents. When they got to Mr. and Mrs. Luce's house, they all got out of the car and went to the door. They let Emma knock on the door.

Mr. Luce answered the door and said, "Come in," and then yelled "Honey, come to the living room! Emily and Ryan is here!" while Mrs. Luce was coming the four of them sat in the living room talking.

Mrs. Luce came in and said, "Hello" to everyone.

Emily said, "Mom, Dad, I would like you to meet Emma and she is part of the family now!"

Mrs. Luce said, "Wait right there, Emma I have something for you!" Mrs. Luce went into the guest room and grabbed a doll and went back to the living room and gave it to Emma and said, "That doll was Emily's when she was your age."

Emma said, "Thank you," to Mrs. Luce and went off and started to play with it while they all visited. Four hours later, the three of them went home and went to bed.

Chapter Seventeen

The Honeymoon

 It was now January. While Ryan was working, Emily was packing the stuff they would be taking on their honeymoon trip to Hawaii. It took Emily about three days to pack. On the third day, they called Ryan's mother.

She picked up and said, "Hello, Son."

"Hello Mother. Can you give us a ride to the airport, and can you watch Emma while we are on the honeymoon?"

"Sure, Son. I will be over in ten minutes."

"Thanks!" They hung up the phones. He told Emma to get

ready for Grandma's house. Emma ran up the stairs and started to pack for Grandma's house. Emily followed behind her to make sure she got everything she needed. Then, there was a ring, and it was the doorbell. Ryan opened the door, and it was his mother.

She asked Ryan, "Where my granddaughter?"

"Emma is up in her room packing to go to your house."

"OK. Well, here the keys, and I'm going upstairs to see her." Ryan took the keys, and his mother went to Emma's room. Emily came down to get a drink of water, and Ryan was almost done loading the car. When the car was packed with everyone's stuff, Ryan's mother took them to the airport.

Once at the airport, Ryan took out their stuff, and they both kissed Emma good-bye and said, "We will see you in a week! Have fun at Grandma's house!"

"OK, I will!" Then, Ryan and Emily went inside to check in for the flight. After about thirty minutes, they heard their flight name, and they boarded the plane. twenty minutes later, the flight attendant was going over the safety protocols, so everyone knew where everything was, in case of an emergency. During this time, the flight attendant was talking, and he had everyone laughing, because he was doing Disney voices. He did a great job of talking, so people mind wouldn't be nervous about flying.

Emily looked at her husband, and said, "I love you so much."

Ryan didn't say anything and just gave her a long kiss. Then they heard the plot say, "Attention passengers! This is your pilot. We will be taking off in about ten minutes. Please have your phones turned off until we get into the air. This flight will take about eight hours. So sit back, relax and enjoy the trip." The pilot had everyone laughing to the point they were crying, all because he was talking in the Disney characters. Ten minutes passed, and the plane started to take off. Now, that they were in the sky, the flight attendant was walking around with drinks and food. Emily brought her lab-top out and was playing games while Ryan was watching the movie that was playing.

After about three hours, they were getting hungry, so Emily asked the flight attendant, "Sir, what do you have to eat on this flight?"

"Well, ma'am, we have some Mahi-Mahi, chicken, or steak. What would you like?"

"I think I would have the Mahi-Mahi," said Emily.

"OK, ma'am, and sir, would you like something?"

"I think I will have the steak," said Ryan.

"OK, sir, and it will be ready in about thirty minutes," and the flight attendant walked off.

Emily asked Ryan, "Dear, what movie are you watching?"

"It's called *Sully*."

"OK." She put her arm through his arm and laid her head on his shoulder. They lost track of time, because the flight attendant came up with their food.

They put the table down, and the flight attendant put the food down on the table and asked them, "Would you like anything to drink with your meal?"

"What do you have?"

"Well, we have beer, wine, water, juice, or soda."

"What kind of wine?"

"We have Pinot Noir or Merlot."

Emily said, "I will take the Pinot Noir."

Ryan said, "I will take the Merlot."

"OK." The flight attendant walked away. A minutes later,

the flight attendant came back and gave them the wine. Ryan and Emily ate their meals and slipped their wine. After they were done, the flight attendant took their plates, and Emily fell asleep. Emily had only been asleep for an hour when she woke up to the rocking of the plane. The pilot came over the intercom, saying everything was fine and it was just some wind. Then, the pilot said to the co pilot, some funny jokes he had heard sometime back.

Everyone calmed down and wasn't nervous anymore, because everyone was laughing too much. About four hours later, they heard the pilot come on the intercom and say, "Welcome to Hawaii! We will be landing in about ten minutes." He said all that in the voice of *Stitch*. The plane was now down on the ground, and everyone had gotten off. Ryan and Emily headed to get their bags and headed to the hotel to check in. When they got to the hotel, they saw the beautiful flowers and were just amazed at how nice the hotel was. They walked into the hotel and checked into their room. Now that they were in their room, they dropped off their bags and headed to a place to get some food. As they walked down the street, they came across a really nice seafood restaurant named *The Seafood Ohana*, and they walked in.

A lady came up and said, "Welcome to *The Seafood Ohana*, where we have all kinds of seafood, and we treat you like family. Just the two of you?"

"Yes."

"Please come with me, and I will take you to your table." They followed the lady to their table and sat down. The lady handed them a few menus and asked, "Would you like anything to drink?"

"Do you have wine here?"

"Yes, we do. We have red and white wine."

"I will have some red wine," said Emily.

Ryan said, "I will have the white wine." The lady took down the information and left. They looked over the menu to see what they wanted . After ten minutes, the lady came back with the wine and crab cakes and shrimp spring rolls.

Emily asked, "What is this for?"

"It's complementary from the restaurant. Are you ready to order?"

"Yes, I will take the King salmon," said Emily.

"soup or salad?"

"clam chowder."

"OK, and what would you like, sir?"

"I would like the king cut Black Angus prime rib with clam chowder." After the lady finished writing everything down, she collected the menus and walked off. While waiting for their food, they were talking about what they were going to be doing tomorrow.

Thirty minutes later, the lady came back with the food and sat it down and said, "Enjoy! Would you like a refill on the wine?"

They both said, "Sure." They started to eat their dinner, and five minutes later, the lady brought their wine to them. When they were done, they paid their bill and walked back to the hotel. They got to the hotel and got comfortable and put on a movie. After about fifteen minutes, Emily had fallen asleep, and Ryan set his phone for 5:00 A.M., the next day, then fell asleep in the middle of the movie.

They got woken up at 5:00 A.M., when Ryan's phone went

off, and they got up. While Emily was in the shower, Ryan was

making coffee for the two of them. After the coffee was made,

Ryan walked into the shower with Emily. Emily and Ryan kissed

and messed around for about thirty minutes in the shower before

they got out and got ready for the day. Emily poured them some

coffee and left the hotel. They took a cab to the Kona Coffee

Farm tour. When they got to the Kona Coffee Farm, they paid for

tickets for the tour. On the tour, the guy talked about the history

of the coffee and what kinds of coffee they had there. The tour

lasted five hours, and Emily wanted to get some coffee before

they left. While Emily was in line to check out.

Ryan walked up to one of the workers there and asked,

"What kind of night shows do you have here?"

"Well, their is the Luau Kalamaku show tonight."

"Luau Kalamaku show?"

"The Luau Kalamaku show is a unique tropical show on the

experience of Kauai. The Luau Kalamaku is just the thing, and

they have a buffet there, too. You two would love the show!"

"Thank you. I will surprise my wife with it." and Ryan

walked back over to Emily, who was almost done paying for the coffee. They left and headed back into town and looked around for a while. Then, they went back to the hotel room to drop off the stuff they got.

Ryan said, "Dear, I have a surprise for you, so wear something nice!"

"OK!" She put on a nice dress, and they headed over to the show that Ryan was told about. When they got there, they were greeted in an old Hawaiian style. Ryan paid the lady, and both of them were seated for the show in ten minutes. The speaker of the show came onto the stage and gave the highlights on the show tonight.

He said, "Tonight's show will be three and a half hours of entertainment at the Hawaiian luau, with an authentic Hawaiian experience: graceful hula dancers, Kilohana rhythms, fantastic music, fire poi twirlers, traditional fire knife dance. So let's get on with the show! Here is the Hawaiian Luau." While the speaker walked off the stage, the Hawaiian Luau came out. They were wearing grass skirts and started doing their dance. This went on for a bit, until the graceful hula dancers came out to dance with them. After several different dances, the speaker came on as they were walking off the stage.

The speaker said, "We are going to take a fifteen break, and the buffet is ready. Thank you." He left the stage.

Ryan and Emily got up and got into the buffet line to get some food. They saw that their were salads that came with two dressings, including Papaya Seed Dressing and Balsamic Vinaigrette, Potato Macaroni Salad, Vegetarian Tofu Salad, and Seasonal Fruit Platter. The entrees were POI, Taro Rolls, Teriyaki Chicken, Steamed Jasmine Rice, Kalua Pork, Vegetable Chow Mein, Hawaiian Mashed Purple Sweet Potatoes, Thai Curry Ratatouille, Fresh Island Caught Fish. The desserts were Rice Pudding with Dark Rum Sauce, Banana Cream Tart, Pineapple Upside Down Cake, Haupia.

After fifteen minutes, the speaker came back out and said, "Are you ready for the second act?" Everyone cheered!

"Yes!"

"Here's what you all have been waiting for! It's the fire poi ball twirlers and the fire knife dancers!" The speaker left the stage. Then, the music started playing, and the fire poi ball twirlers and the fire knife dancers came out. They had everyone cheering, the whole time they were performing. When it was over, Ryan and Emily went back to the hotel. Once in the hotel room, they changed into their sleep wear and just passed out, because their bellies were full, and they were really tried.

The next morning, they slept in until eight that morning, and then they got up. They looked at each other, and Ryan said, "What you want to do today?"

"We could go on the Atlantis submarines on Maui and then, after that, go shopping?"

"OK, that sounds good!" They got ready and headed over to the place. Once they got to the Atlantis submarines, Maui, they bought some tickets and then got onto the submarine. They only had to wait twenty minutes before they left the port and went out to sea.

The Captain came on and told everyone, "We are about to dive under the water," and everyone went to the windows to see the stuff under the ocean. After a few minutes, Emily saw some small colorful fish, and she took some pictures of some Parrot Fish, Pennant Butterfly-fish, and Hawaiian Cleaner Wrasse. About thirty minutes later, they saw some sunken ships, along with some Gray Reef sharks, Spotted Eagle Ray , and a Manta Ray. Then they moved in a different direction, and they saw some Humpback Whales and Dolphins. All of a sudden, out of nowhere, a White striped Octopus lock itself onto a window like it wanted a ride but let go after about ten minutes. On the way back, they saw some Hawks-bill Sea Turtles and Hawaiian Green Sea Turtles. Now, they were coming into the port to dock, and after they docked, everyone got off the submarine.

Ryan turned to Emily and asked, "Did you have fun on that?"

"Yes, I really enjoyed it. I had gotten lots of pictures of everything and can't wait to show Emma when we get home!"

"I'm happy you are enjoying yourself! It's been a long time since you have been this happy."

"That is not true!"

"What do you mean?"

"When I found you, I was happy." Ryan didn't say a word after that but just pulled Emily really close to him and give her a long kiss. Then, they left the dock and did some shopping. While they were walking, Emily found the shells and clothing store and went in. She had seen a very cute flower dress for Emma and some shell necklaces. She took them to the front counter to pay for them, and then they left the store. They both started to get hungry and found a sushi restaurant called *Hawaiian Water Sushi*, so they walked in.

The hostess said, "Aloha, and welcome to the *Hawaiian Water Sushi* and we have the best sushi in town. Is it for two?"

"Yes."

"Come this way." They followed the hostess to their table and sat down. Then, she asked, "May I get you something to drink?"

"Hot tea and a Dr Pepper," said Ryan, and the hostess walked off. Ryan and Emily looked at the menu, and Ryan asked, Emily, "What looks good to you?"

"Let see. The Rainbow Roll and a steak look good. What are you going to get?"

"I was thinking the steak too, along with the Baked Dynamite."

"Sounds good."

Then, the hostess came with the drinks and Ryan said, "We

are ready to order."

"OK. Let me get you someone," and she walked off.

A few minutes later a waiter came by and said, "My name is Brandon, and I will be your waiter for the evening. Ma'am, what would you like to have?"

"I would like a Rainbow Roll and the Sirloin Steak."

"How would you like your steak prepared?"

"Medium rare."

"Would you like soup or salad?"

"Salad."

"OK, we have Blue Cheese and Hawaiian Pineapple balsamic."

"Hawaiian Pineapple balsamic."

"OK, and what can I get for you, sir?"

"I will take the Baked Dynamite, medium rare sirloin steak, salad with blue cheese."

"OK," said the waiter, who went back over the order and asked if everything was correct and they said, "yes."

"OK, thank you." Brandon walked away.

Ryan and Emily talked about what they want to do

tomorrow and Emily said, " What about we have fun all night long and go on the North Shore beach tour when we wake up?" The whole time she was saying that, her foot was playing with Ryan under the table.

"I think that's a good idea," Ryan said with a smile on his face, and Emily put her foot down when the food had got there. They talked some more while they ate. After they were done, they paid for the meals and went back to the hotel at around seven that night. While they were walking into the hotel room, they acted like a couple of horny teenagers in high school, because clothing got thrown everywhere in that hotel room. They finally fell asleep around three in the morning.

They woke up around noon and started getting ready for that North Shore beach tour.

Ryan told Emily, "You wore me out last night."

Emily just giggled for a few minutes and then said, "I know I did," and giggled some more. When they were ready, they headed to where the tour was. Once they got their, they bought some tickets and got on the tour car. The whole time on the tour, Emily took so many pictures that she filled two SD cards and was working on the third one. She was just trying to remember the trip, because she and Emma going to make a scrapbook when they got back home. They saw temples, some endangered bird species, and a turtle beach where the green turtles were. The tour stayed there so everyone could watch the sunset, and after that, they all loaded up and came back where they started.

On the way back, Emily said, "I got great pictures of the sunset."

"Did you use a whole SD card?" Ryan asked laughing.

In a playful way, Emily said, "Shut up!" and Emily was laughing, because Ryan was tickling her.when they got back, they headed back to the hotel to pack up for the flight home the next day and to get some sleep.

At six in the morning, they woke up and headed for breakfast. After they were done with breakfast, they went back to the hotel and got their stuff. On the way out, they checked out and headed to the airport. They arrived at the airport, and they checked in. After thirty minutes, they boarded the plane, and after forty minutes, the plane took off. They arrived back in Texas and everyone got off the plane after it landed. Ryan and

Emily got their bags and went outside to see Ryan's mom waiting for them.

On the way to the house, Emma asked,

"How was your trip, Mommy and Daddy?"

"We had a great time, and I have lots of pictures," said Emily.

"Ya, now we can do the scrapbook!" After about twenty minutes, they returned to their home. Ryan took the bags in, and Emma, Ryan's mom, and Emily started to make some dinner. When dinner was over, Emma went and played while everyone else talked until it was time for Emma to go to bed. Ryan's mom left, and Ryan went up to their room, while Emily was getting Emma ready for bed. After that Emma was asleep, Emily walked into their room, and Ryan was sound asleep, so Emily got into her bed wear and went to bed for the night.

Chapter Eighteen

Baby Fever

Ryan and Emily talked, and they both agreed, "We are ready to have a baby." They called the New Horizons Medical Center and made an appointment for the next day to see the doctor.

When they got to the doctor's office, the front window lady said, "Welcome, and how may I help you?"

"I'm here to see the doctor."

"What your name?"

"My name is Emily."

"There you are. Please fill out these papers." After about

ten minutes, Emily was done filling out the paperwork. She took it back up to the window and the lady at the window said, "It will be about fifteen minutes." Emily took a seat.

Fifteen minutes passed, and she heard the lady call out, "Emily."

Ryan and Emily got up and walked to the lady, where she took them to the waiting room. Then, she told them, "The doctor will be in shortly,"and she shut the door.

After fifteen minutes, the doctor walked into the room and said, "Hello, Emily. How many I help you?"

"Hi, Doc! My husband and I want to have a baby."

"OK, then let's take a look at you and get some more information from you." After about five minutes of examining Emily, he asked, "Have you had any surgery?"

"Yes, I had gender reassignment surgery sometime back."

"OK, that tells me a lot. In Vitro Fertilization, or (IVF), for short, will be a 50/50 chance of taking."

"We know, and we are willing to take the chance."

"OK, I will be giving you fertility medications and some of the side effects of it includes headaches, mood swings, abdominal pain and bloating, and rare Ovarian Hyper-stimulation

Syndrome or (OHSS). Some risks associated with (OHSS) would

be nausea or vomiting, decreased urinary frequency, shortness of

breath, faintness, severe stomach pains and bloating, and ten

pounds weight gain within three to five days. I will see you in a

month. Ryan, I will need a sample of your sperm from you to put

with the eggs."

The doctor wrote the prescription out for Emily and Ryan,

and Emily left the room. Ryan went and did what the doctor

asked, and when he was done, he gave it to the nurse. Ryan was

waiting for Emily while she was making an appointment to see

the doctor in a month. Then, they left the office. Emily walked

up to the car and got in, and they went home.

After a month went by, Ryan and Emily went back to see

the doctor. Emily got checked in, and they were waiting to be

called by the nurse, to go back. Ten minutes later, Emily got

called, and they went back and were waiting for the doctor.

Five minutes later, the doctor came in and said, "Hi, Emily

and Ryan. I have three eggs for you, and it won't take long to put

them in, and you're be on your way. Keep taking the medication, because it will help them to take to you. The high risk symptoms are heavy vaginal bleeding, pelvis, blood in the urine, or a fever of a hundred point five Fahrenheit (thirty-eight Celsius). If any of those things occur, call me immediately. Some other mild side effects you might have include passing a small amount of fluid (may be clear or blood-tinged) after the procedure, mild cramping and bloating, constipation, and breast tenderness. They are normal during the IVF."

"OK, Doctor. Thank you so much." The doctor finished up his paperwork and told them they could go, they left and went home.

A month later, Emily woke up in the morning. She got out of bed slowly, to try not to wake Ryan up. She went into the kitchen to make some coffee and make some eggs for breakfast. She got some eggs and broke two eggs into a bowl and started to beat them. Then, she added some milk,salt, and some black pepper. She poured the eggs in the pan and started to cook them. All of a sudden, she felt like throwing up and turned off the stove and ran to the bathroom. She threw up once in the toilet. This lasted for about fifteen minutes but felt like thirty minutes. When she wasn't throwing up anymore, she went back into the kitchen and saw the eggs and lost her appetite. As she was tossing out the eggs, the smell of the eggs got to her again, and she ran back into the bathroom to throw up again. While she was in the bathroom, she thought to herself, *"Can I be pregnant?"* So she left for the store to get a pregnancy test. She got to the store and got the test, paid for it, and then went into the store bathroom and took the test.

She waited the time, allotted and when she saw it, it had two lines on it which meant positive for being pregnant. She left the store and while she was walking to the car, she called her doctor to make an appointment to see if it was a true positive and not a faulty test.

The doctor's office picked up and said, "Thank you for calling New Horizons Medical Center. How may I help you?" the lady asked.

"I need an appointment with the doctor," said Emily.

"Well, we have an opening at 2:00 P.M. today," said the lady.

"That great, and I'll see you then," said Emily.

"OK, we will see you then, Emily," said the lady and Emily drove home. Three hours later, she left for the doctor's appointment. She got to the doctor and checked in. Ten minutes later, she got called back. The nurse check the pre-screening and took her to a room, where Emily waited for the doctor.

The doctor came in about ten minutes later and asked Emily, "So what brings you here today, Emily?"

"I think the eggs might have took hold, and I might be pregnant."

"OK, let me draw some blood, and test it." With that, the doctor left, and a nurse came in and drew some of Emily's blood for testing. After about fifteen minutes, the doctor came back and said, "Well according to the blood test, it shows that you are pregnant. Congratulations, Emily."

"Thank you, doctor." Emily walked out and went home.

When she got home, Ryan asked, "Is everything OK?"

"Yes, dear. I just had a check up with the doctor and everything is good."

"That is good." Ryan went into the living room to watch some TV. Emily was in the kitchen making dinner for the night.

After an hour, Emily put her husband's favorite food on the table. Then she called for her husband and Emma to the table.

While they was eating dinner, Emily said, "Dear, I have some news for you."

"What kind of news do you have? Does it have to do with the doctor you went and saw today?" said Ryan.

"Yes, and I am four weeks pregnant!" said Emily.

"That is great news!" said Ryan.

"Yea, I hope your ready to raise four kids, because all three eggs took!" said Emily, and Ryan didn't say anything for about five minutes.

"Is everything OK, dear?" asked Emily.

"Yeah, I was just thinking about something," said Ryan.

"What you thinking about?" asked Emily.

"If we have a big enough room for three kids and baby stuff," said Ryan.

"Oh, OK, we can see about that later," said Emily.

"Mommy, am I going to have sisters or brothers?" asked Emma.

"Sweetie, it's too early to find that out, but when I know, I will tell you," said Emily.

"OK, Mommy," said Emma.

When dinner was over, Emma went into the living room and started watching TV, while Ryan and Emily were cleaning up.

After the clean up was done, Emily told Emma, "Sweetie, it's time to get clean up for bed." Emma got up and turned the TV off and did what her mom said. When Emma got done with her shower and got her kitty pajamas on, she got into bed. Then ten minutes later, Emily came in to read a story to her until she fell asleep. After Emma was asleep, Emily walked out of the room and went to the living room. She sat next to her husband and snuggled up to him.

Then he told her, "I have something for you, but you don't get it until six months from now." Emily snuggled harder until she fell asleep after about thirty minutes, with her husband's arm around her.

Chapter Nineteen

Full of Surprises

 On Tuesday morning, Emily had a six month check up at around nine in the morning, so she woke up around 6:00 A.M., because it takes her a while to get ready for the day. It's around 8:15 A.M., and she left the house to go to her appointment. Once she got there she got of the car and walked to the doctor's office. Now that she was in the office, she checked in. It had been fifteen minutes, and the nurse called her name, so she walked back into the room. Now she was in the room and had got on the table. The nurse left and brought back an ultrasound in to take a look at the

baby. When the nurse put some gel and then the transducer onto Emily's stomach, they saw all three of the little babies.

Then ask Emily, "Would you like to see the babies?"

"Yes." So she turned the monitor towards Emily, so Emily could see them. She started to tear up.

The nurse asked, "Why are you crying?"

"It's always been my dream to carry and have a baby," and with what Emily said, the nurse almost tear up herself.

Then nurse asked, "Would you like to know the sex?"

"Sure!" said Emily.

"Well, there is one girl and two boys." Emily started crying, and the nurse asked, "What wrong?"

"I'm hoping my kids don't have to go though, what I had to go through growing up," and this put a puzzled look on the nurse's face.

"What do you mean?"

"I was a boy until the age of twenty-six. I had a gender reassignment surgery. I just hope my children can live normal lives, but if it happens, I will still love them, no matter what."

"When did you know?"

"I knew when I was ten years old."

"Sorry, I don't mean to pry into your personal life."

"Its OK. The tone of your voice told me you didn't know. I will have a baby shower soon, and I can call you with the day and time if you would like to come."

"That would be great, and I can't wait!"

Then the doctor came in and said, "Hello, Emily, and how are we doing today?"

"I'm doing good."

"That's good." He turned to the nurse and asked, "What did the ultrasound look like?"

"Everything looking good!"

"That's good, and now, Emily I need to look inside to see if everything is good down there and take a few samples."

"OK, Doc." Then the doctor looked around down there, and the nurse brought some cotton swabs over. He took one and rubbed it on the outside of the opening and another just inside.

Emily asked, "I'm just wondering, what are you looking for?"

"We are just making sure there is no infection."

"OK,"

Then the doctor said, "OK, Emily, we are all done. How is it going at home?"

"Well, my legs have been swelling."

"Well, I'm ordering you more bed rest, with your feet slightly elevated."

"OK, Doc."

"Well, we are done here." Then the doctor told the nurse to finished up here and he walked out the door. The nurse finished up and handed the papers and a picture of the ultrasound. Then, Emily left the office and went home. Once she got home, she went up to her room to lay down and watch some TV before she fell asleep. She awoke five hours later, when Ryan came home.

A few minutes later, Ryan came up to the room and asked, "How was the check up?"

"It went well, and I found out what we are having. Would you like to know now or when we do the revealing party?"

"I can wait until the revealing party."

"OK, set it up!"

"OK." Ryan got into bed with Emily and pulled her to him,

so he could hold her. They both fell asleep with each other in their arms.

The day came for the revealing party, and Ryan been working hard for a week. He called family and friends. They were going to show up around 5:00 P.M.

Emily said, "What are we going to do for food?"

"I told everyone it's a potluck and to bring their favorite dish."

"OK, and where is the stuff we going to reveal with?"

"That's in the house, waiting for you," and Emily went inside to put the colors into all three boxes.

Then walked out and told Ryan, "Dear, the box's are ready."

"OK." Ryan took them outside and set them up. Now it was 5:00 P.M., and everyone was showing up. They came out into the backyard and sat the food on the table. They talked for about thirty minutes before they all started to eat. After everyone was done eating, it was now time for the revealing of what they are going to have. Ryan was just about to pull the rope, and Emma was pulling on Ryan's shirt and saying, "Can I do it?" and Ryan looked at her.

Then she pleaded, "Please, Daddy!"

"OK, sweetie , here you go!" and he handed Emma the rope. She pulled the rope as hard as her little hand could pull and the balloons came out. There were two boxes with blue balloons, and the last one had pink balloons in it.

The look on Emma's face was priceless and she said, "You mean, I have two brothers and a sister!"

"Yes, baby and I know you are going to be a great big sister to all of them," said Emily, and everyone was clapping.

Some of the friends and family asked Emily, "When is the baby shower going to be?"

"Three weeks from now." Now, everyone started to eat ice cream and cake.

When that was all over, Ryan told Emily, "You can go lay down, and I will clean up out here."

"Are you sure?"

"Yeah. I have my little helper right here."

Emma looks up and says, "Yeah, I'm Daddy's little helper."

"OK!" Emily walked up to their bedroom and lay down.

About an hour later, Ryan had cleaned up and had Emma in bed before coming into the room where he found Emily asleep. He turned the TV off, lay down in bed, and he fell asleep himself.

Three weeks had passed, and it's time for the baby shower. A lot of people showed up with lots of gifts. Ryan had to put some of the gifts in the kitchen, because they ran out of room in the living room, due to all the people that showed up.

After everyone had sat down, they were talking, while Emily was opening the gifts. Some of the items she got were clothing, bottles, baby wipes and diapers. Some got her some baby stuff like a crib and car seat. This went on for a few hours, and Emily had a lot of fun. After thanking everyone for coming, it took about thirty minutes before everyone had left, and Emily was feeling tired, so she went up to her room to go to sleep.

About a week later, Ryan came up to Emily and said, "Be ready by 4:00 P.M., because I'm going to take you somewhere."

"OK." Ryan left for work. All day Emily thought about what it could be: could it be dinner, dancing, or a movie? She thought, *I really hates when he does this to me.* She cleaned the house and by the time, she was done cleaning, it was time to get ready for whatever he had planned. Now, it was 4:00 P.M., and Ryan pulled up to the house, all dressed up with flowers in his hand. Emily thought it might be dinner if he dressed at the office for this and brought her flowers. They got in the car, and an hour later, they showed up at a really big building. They parked and walked up to the big building. Ryan handed the tickets to the person and went into the building. Then, they went to their seats that were stated on the tickets and sat down at a table.

Emily asked, "So, Mister, who are we going to see?"

"You will find out!"

The waitress came by and asked, "Would you like some drinks?"

"I will take a Bud Light," Ryan said.

Emily said, "Dr Pepper," and the waitress left.

About ten minutes later, a guy came out on stage and asked, "How is everyone doing tonight? I know you been waiting a lifetime for them to come to Texas for the first time. So I will stop talking, so you can hear what you have been waiting for, the country boy band from Georgia, called The Lacs." Everyone cheered when they came out.

The lead person said, "Welcome, Texas! We are happy to be here in this big wonderful state. So, let's get started with the song, "*God Bless a Country Girl!*" When that was done, they went into the song, *Kicking Up Mud.* People got on the dance floor and were dancing the two step and line dancing. When the band took a break, the people started to bring out the dinner that was offered with the tickets. The dinner was a prime rib, baked potato, corn and bread roll.

The band came back out and said, "We want to do the songs, but, we can't do it without our very good friend, and we all know who that is!"

The crowd of people chanted the name Colt Ford, over and over and cheered when he came out on stage. "Let's kick it off with the song *Shindig* or *Field Party?*" and everyone chanted *Shindig!*

"OK, Colt, you heard them!"

"I think I heard they wanted the song *Field Party,*" Colt Ford said.

"I think I heard the something else," and he gave Colt a wink and told the band, *Field Party,* while winking at them too.

Everyone "booed" when they said that, but when they started to play, they all cheered, because they all realized that the band was joking with everyone. When the band The Lacs was done with the two songs, they gave the stage to Colt Ford and his band. When Colt Ford were done, everyone started to leave the building and go home. While they were going home Emily said, "Thank you, dear, I had a good time tonight."

"That's good to hear, because I have been planning this night for a while now, and it's not over yet!"

"Oh, what else you have in mind?"

"You will see when we get home."

"OK, give me a hint."

"Well, your hint is that my mother has Emma all night." Emily was thinking in her head, *That she hate it, but loves it, all the same time, when Ryan, did this type of stuff.* So they got home, Emily had an idea what it might be. She walked up to their room and changed from what she was wearing that night into her blue lace two piece lingerie that barely covered anything, then got into bed to wait for her man. Ryan came up to the bedroom with some strawberries and whip cream. Emily was thinking in your head, *Somehow, I know what he was hinting at on the way home.*" Ryan got into bed with his underwear on and saw what Emily had on. Then, from that point on, things got heated for a good two to three hours, before they both fell asleep with each other in their arms.

Chapter Twenty

Birthday of Three

It was just a normal Friday morning, and Emma with Ryan's mother for the day. Emily was cleaning the house, while Ryan was outside cleaning the backyard. When she was done cleaning the house two hours later, she felt like she had to use the bathroom. So as she was walking to it, a lot of water just went everywhere in the hallway. The weather started to change. The wind started to pick up fast, and Ryan came into the house to hear Emily yelling for him.

He ran to her asking, "What wrong, honey?"

"I think it might be time to go to the hospital, because my water just broke!"

Ryan started to freak out, then said, "No, not now, not today!"

"Yes, it's time."

"No, no, no!"

"Why do you keep saying that"

"The wind just started to blow, and it's getting faster!"

"Oh, I know, but just get to the hospital fast but safe!"

"OK."

Ryan helped Emily to the car and start driving to the hospital.

Then Emily said, "We forgot the bag!"

"I will go back for it later. Right now, we need to get you to the hospital!" By now, the wind was really blowing. It's was thundering and lightning too. About halfway to the hospital, it started hailing and Ryan said, "This is not a really good sign."

"Looks like a tornado is about to form."

"That what I was thinking, too," said Ryan, and there was some lightning off in the distance hitting the ground. They were both praying they get to the hospital safely. About twenty minutes later, they made it to the hospital, and Ryan drove up to the ER doors. Ryan got out of the car and ran inside to get someone to bring a wheelchair for Emily. While Ryan was doing that, there was an ambulance honking it's horn, because they were in the way.

When Ryan and the nurse came out with the wheelchair, the ambulance driver said, "Why don't you get that junk car out of here, so I can do my job?" Ryan ignored the guy, because he was worried about his wife.

The nurse said, "You can go around."

"Screw you bitch! Make that guy move that piece of shit car out of my way!"

Now, they were both not listening to the idiot. They got Emily into the wheelchair, and the nurse wheeled her inside the hospital to get her logged in. Before Ryan moved his car to go park it, he wrote down the ambulance information, and then he parked his car. He got out of the car and went into the hospital.

Emily saw him. She waved and said, "Ryan, over here!"

He heard her and walked over to sit next to her. After about ten minutes, Emily was being called to the back, and the nurse said, "We have called your doctor, and we are going to get you a room." Emily follow her to the back, Ryan called the company of the ambulance, and a guy picked up the phone and said, "Hello, thanks for calling Spirit Ambulance, and how may I help you?"

"Can I speak to your boss, please?"

"Sure, just hold on a moment, and I will get her." A few minutes later, the guy said, "Sir, I'm sending you to her now."

Then Ryan heard a lady voice said, "Hello, my name is Allison, and I'm the manager here. How may I help you?"

"While I was in the ER area next to the doors at the hospital, your driver was honking his horn wildly, calling me and the nurse names. He told me to move my piece of shit car out of his way, and I was there because my wife is going to give birth to triplets."

" I'm sorry about that, sir, and do you have the information of the ambulance?"

"Yes, the license plate is J759908, and the vehicle number is 4856. The guy is about in his last twenty's or early thirty's, white skin and about medium build."

All Ryan heard was, "shoot, not that guy again!" She said, "Thank you for letting me know."

"Sounds like you have been having a lot of problems with that guy."

"Yes, and I will take care of this."

"You're welcome, and you have a nice day."

"You too, and I will, and you and your wife, good luck!"

"Thanks." They both hung up the phone, and Ryan went to his wife's hospital room. When he got into the room, Emily had the news on. The news was saying that a hurricane hit Galveston ten minutes earlier, causing massive amount of flooding, killing seventy-eight people and wounding over two hundred. Tornadoes were forming in Houston, which could make the power go out in some places. Emily was getting worried now. Ryan told Emily, "Things are going to be OK."

"What is going to happen if the lights go out? Remember, I am getting a C-Section!"

Just then, her doctor came in and said, "Hello, Emily. I see they are ready to come out."

"Yes, doctor they are."

"Well, let's get you in the operating room to do the C-Section, and get them out of you." So they got the operating room ready. They got Emily and took her to the room. As soon has they got in, their lights started to flicker off and on. Then, they felt the ground move and knew it was an earthquake. They waited for twenty minutes to see if it would stop, and it did, for moment.

The doctor said, "I'm going to give you a shot of anesthesia, and you will be numb from the waist down. You will still be awake, okay?"

"OK, Doctor. Let's get this going, because I want to see my babies!" The doctor gave Emily the shot, and they waited for about thirty minutes to allow the shot to work before starting the C-Section. After the thirty minutes, the doctor started the surgery. The surgery lasted for about an hour and a half to deliver all three babies and Emily back into her room were she fell asleep.

The next morning, Emily woke up and the nurse showed Emily her babies. She let Emily hold them one at a time, so Emily wouldn't rip a stitch.

Emily had tears coming from her eyes, and the nurse asked, "Why are you crying?"

"Because I'm happy, and I waited my whole life to carry my own kids."

Then, Ryan walked into the room and said, "Hey, dear!"

"Hey, hun, did you get the chance to see are little ones?"

"Yes, and I love all of you! Someone is here to see you." He walked out of the room and came back with his mother and Emma.

Emily said, "Thank you for watching my baby girl."

"You don't have to thank me, because I enjoy my granddaughter."

"OK. Emma, come give mommy a hug!" Emma ran over and gave Emily a hug. After the hug, she introduced Emma to her two brothers, Shawn and Troy and her sister, Amber. After about a week in the hospital, the doctor released Emily. It was okay to go home. So Emily got ready and got all three little ones ready. They got the paperwork and walked to the car. They got in and went home.

Once they got home, Ryan said, "I will carry the boys in,

and I will get everything else, so you can go relax with the babies"

"OK," Emily did that while Ryan brought everything in.

Chapter Twenty-One

The Ranch

Emily recovered from the C-Section surgery of the three kids, after about a month. Ryan and Emily bought a one hundred thousand acre ranch, with a six bedroom, three bath house and twenty thousand acres with forest outside Sweetwater, Wyoming. When they were ready to move in to the house, Luke and Mr. Luce were helping Ryan and moved the stuff into the house while Emily and Mrs. Luce watched Emma playing with Troy. When Luke and Ryan were moving the gun cabinet into the house, Luke said to Ryan, "I haven't seen that old thing since it was at your grandpa's place."

Ryan said, "Yea when Grandpa passed, my grandma gave it to me, it's because she knew I love it."

Luke said, "That was nice of your grandma to do that."

"Hey Ryan, what are your plans to do with all this land?" asked Mr. Luce.

"Well, Emily and I were thinking about having a cattle ranch with a small Christian camp on it and working with the local county cops and CPS to be a foster care, too."

"Oh, cool, Ryan, and if you need help with anything, let me know," said Mr. Luce.

Now, the U-Haul was empty, and it was about dinner time, so Ryan said to everyone there, "Dinner is on us." They all went to the local restaurant, where they had a good time. After that, everyone spent the night at the house, and in the morning, Luke, Mr. and Mrs. Luce left to go back to Texas.

As days went by Ryan continued working on putting the fences up for the cattle, cutting down some wood in the forest and making a path through it. He wanted to still keep the beauty of the forest. In the forest, in the spot he had cut down, he made a little campground and then made a thinking area with a cover. Then Ryan ordered some wood and pipe to make a barn, horse stables, a rabbit hut, and a carport. The next day, while Ryan was building those things, Emily and Emma were inside the house, decorating the rooms. Emma's room was being painted a light blue with pink curtains, and the babies nursery had a lot of country in it. It was now getting dark, and Ryan got some of the things done but would need help to build the barn. The next morning Ryan, went into town to see if he could find some people to help him, and he went to the coffee shop where, back home, if you needed help, the coffee shop was the place to go.

When he walked in, there was a board on the left where people put things up, so Ryan put up a paper that said, "Help on building a barn needed! Will feed and pay for help too." He put his call number on the flyer, then went to the counter and ordered some coffee. After about two hours drinking coffee, Ryan decided to go home. Emily called and asked him to stop and pick up a few things at the store before coming home. He did and then went home for the night. The next morning, Ryan called around to find a good price on ten thousand head of cattle and as soon as he got off the phone, the phone rung.

Ryan picked up and said, "Hello."

The other person said, "Hello, my name is Steve, and is this Ryan?

Ryan said, "Yes, this is he. How may I help you?"

The guy said, Well I'm calling about the paper at the coffee shop about the barn. Me and my three brothers would like to help you out. We work in construction, and work is slow right now."

Ryan said, "How about you come to the house, say tomorrow morning at around 8:00 A.M.?"

Steve said, "OK, we will see you." Then they both hung up. Then, Ryan called around to find where to get rabbits, and after that, he helped Emily out with the house until it was a bed time.

The next morning, Ryan woke up and got ready and was having some coffee when the guys showed up. Ryan walked outside to greet them, and Steve and his three brothers walked up.

Steve said, "Morning, Ryan. This is Sam, Nemo, and Alex. These are my three brothers."

Ryan said, "It's nice to meet you all." With that, the five

men got to work on the top part of the barn, because Ryan already had dug the hole to the house to the barn and built the bottom of the barn where the cattle were going to stay for the winter. The five men started to build the walls of the barn and the roof. It was now lunch time, because Emily rang the bell, that was outside. When the men got to the house, Emily had lunch on the table, and everyone ate. After lunch was over, the men went back out to start putting up the walls to the barn. It's now about 6:00 P.M.

Ryan said, "Hey, guys. I will cook steak for dinner, and if you like to stay, you can."

The guys said, "Thanks, Ryan." When they got to the house, Ryan fired up the grill that look liked a bull. While Emily seasoned the steak, everyone told Ryan how they like them. Steve told Ryan that it would be a week before they got done with it, and Ryan said, "That would be okay." After dinner, the guys left, and Emily and Ryan cleaned up and went to bed. A week later, the barn was built, and Ryan gave each brother one thousand dollars for all the hard work they did. That same day, Ryan went to the cattle and horse auction, and Ryan brought ten thousand head of Angus cattle and nine quarter horses for the ranch and one older horse for Troy. They would be delivered the next day.

Ryan got home he put an ad in the local newspaper for a foreman and two ranch hands. The next morning, at around 10:00 A.M., the horses showed up, and Ryan put the horses in the barn. Then, while Emily and Emma were watering and feeding the horses, the cattle showed up, and Ryan told the guys that he wanted them in the field, so the delivery guys pulled their trucks over to the field, and they started to unload the cattle into the field. About three days later, a guy called and asked Ryan if the foreman and the ranch hands jobs were still open.

Ryan said, "Yes, they're still open."

That's great. When can we come by? My name is Mace."

Ryan said, "How about right now,"

Mace said, "okay, we will be there."

Ryan said, "See you soon! So, about an hour later, Mace and his two boys showed up, and Ryan saw them arrive and went to meet them.

"Hello, how are you?" asked Ryan.

"I'm good," said Mace. "The other two knuckleheads are my boys Jesse and David." Ryan looked over Mace's resume, and he liked what he saw and hired all three of them. Ryan told Mace they could start in four days and that the job paid one thousand two hundred a month for a foreman and eight hundred a month for a ranch hand. The house over there would be for the hands, and there would not be rent. That the only thing was that they'd have to buy their food and gas for there own cars. The foreman would get their own truck.

So Mace said, "My boys and I will take the job."

Ryan asked, "Mace, if they would like to stay for dinner.

Mace said, "Yes, we will take you up on that! Thank you, Ryan."

While the boys were helping Emily in the kitchen, Ryan and Mace got to talking while Ryan cooked the meat.

Mace said, "Thank you for the jobs."

Ryan said, "No problem!"

Then Mace said, "Ever since my wife passed away, it has been so hard to find a job with flexible hours."

Ryan asked, "What did your wife die of? But if you don't

want to talk about it, I understand."

Mace said, "it's OK." My wife died of cancer last year, and it's been hard ever since then."

"Well, Mace. just think of Emily and me as your family," said Ryan, and Mace started to cry, because of how happy he was to hear that people still had a kind heart. After dinner, Mace, Jesse, and David left and went back to where they were staying.

Over the next four days, Mace and his boys were moving in to the house for the hands, and on the fourth day, they started working on the ranch. While Mace and his boys were working, Ryan started to building a small rodeo arena for when they started the rodeo college scholarships in two years. Ryan got a call from Pastor Roger to see if they could use part of the land for a summer camp that year, because the wild fires had came close to the camp that year and it was not safe for the kids.

Ryan said, "Sure, you can, Roger."

Then, Roger said, "Thank you, and God Bless you," and they both hung up the phone.

The next morning, Ryan started to build an area for the camp and a place where they could put up a tent for worship.

It finally became late in the day, and they were watching the news, and they said that in some parts would be a bad storm and to take safety measures, so Ryan got the hands, and they went over everything. When it was good for the night, then everyone went to bed. Emily woke up around 11:00 P.M., to the heavy storms, and all of a sudden the cell phone rang, and it was the local CPS worker with whom they had worked with, and Emily said, "Hello, Jade. What's wrong?"

Jade said, "Sorry to call you this late, but there has been a big accident on the freeway tonight and the homes are full, and I don't know where to put the six kids tonight. I can tell you more later.

Emily told Jade to bring them to the house. "I will let Ryan know."

Jade said, "thank you, I will be right over there." Emily woke up Ryan and told him that Jade was coming over and told him what had happened. Two hours passed, Jade drove up, and Emily took the kids to the house while Ryan talked to Jade.

"I'm so sorry, Ryan, that I woke you guys up."

Ryan said "Stop, Jade. It's okay Jade. That's what we are

here for. What happened?

Jade said, "Well, there was a big accident on the freeway, and the parents of the three little kids died in the accident, and the other three kids parents are being rushed to the local hospital.

Ryan said, "Okay, they can stay here as long has you need them to."

Jade said, "Thank you." Jade got into the van and left. Ryan went into the house to meet the kids and help them to calm down enough to where they could go to sleep. After they fell asleep Emily and Ryan went back to bed, and Ryan told Emily what all happened and that they had them until Jade knew what to do with them. Then they fell back to sleep.

Over the next few weeks, Jade drove up to the house, and Emily came out, and they talked, and Jade said, "That she was there to pick up three of the kids, because the parents just got out of the hospital."

Emily asked, "What are you guys going to do with the other three kids?"

Jade said, "They only got hold of the family of one of the kids, and they were going to be there in three days. No word of family for the other two kids."

Emily said, "Let's start the paperwork for fostering the other two kids."

Jade said, "okay, give me a few days to get the paperwork filled out for Ryan and you."

So, Emily called Ryan on the cell to bring the three kids that were going with Jade up to the house. Ryan brought up the three kids, and Jade got them in the van with there stuff and left the ranch. Then Jade came back in three days with the other kid's family and they picked her up, and Jade had the paperwork for Emily and Ryan to sign for Aaron and Jasmine, the two that were left out of the six kids that came that night of the accident. That evening, Emily and Ryan told eight year old Aaron and ten year old Jasmine that they were going to stay with them for some time, and they were okay with it.

It had been two years, and the ranch was doing well, so it was time for the Eaglewolf Ranch rodeo. The ranch was named after Bob Cola, the good friend of the family that had passed away while Ryan was in Wyoming. Ryan put flyer's up all over the town and in the newspaper about the scholarships rodeo that was going to be taking place at the ranch in one week. You would have to be a senior and would have to have a signed paper from one's parents to be part of the rodeo. There would be two scholarships, and each scholarship would be two thousand dollars. One went to the top bull rider, and the other one would go to the top in barrels racing. Over the six days, there were forty seniors that put in for the rodeo. There were fifteen bull riders and twenty-five barrel racers. The night of the rodeo came, and the ranch was full of people, and the rodeo took off at 6:00 P.M. and went for a while. At 11:00 P.M., the time came to say who the winners were. Ryan went into the middle of the arena with an envelope from the judges. He opened it and asked for Tony Leaf and Tiffany Wright to please come to the middle of the arena.

Them two came down and Ryan said, "On behalf of Emily and I and the Eaglewolf Ranch grant, Tony Leaf and Tiffany Wright win their two thousand dollars college scholarships. With that everyone applauded for them, and when the rodeo was over, everyone left, and Ryan and the ranch hands cleaned everything up, and then everyone went to bed.

The

End

ABOUT THE AUTHOR

Since the age of 10, Emily Worrell knew that she was different, but she had to hide who she was for 23 years. At the age of 33, she couldn't hide anymore and came out as transgender female. She was kicked out of her house and had to live in her car, and might not have made it without some friends who were there for her. Country love story is based on Emily's hopes, her dreams, and some real-life experiences, and tells the story of a post-op transgender female falling in love with a cowboy and the tests their love endures.

www.ingramcontent.com/pod-product-compliance
Lightning Source LLC
Chambersburg PA
CBHW031335170626
46807CB00002B/711